SWIFT CURRENT

by

Angela Dorsey

www.ponybooks.com

Original Title: Swift Current
Cover Design: 2011 Marina Miller
Printed in the USA, 2011

ISBN: 978-0-9876848-2-0

Enchanted Pony Books
www.ponybooks.com

Horse Guardian Series

Dark Fire
Desert Song
Condor Mountain
Swift Current
Gold Fever
Slave Child
Rattlesnake Rock
Sobekkare's Revenge
Mystic Tide
Silver Dream
Fighting Chance
Wolf Chasm

Freedom Series

Freedom
Echo
Whisper

Whinnies on the Wind Series

Winter of Crystal Dances
Spring of the Poacher's Moon
Summer of Wild Hearts
Autumn in Snake Canyon
Winter of Sinking Waters
Spring of Secrets
Summer of Desperate Races
Autumn of the Angel Mare
Winter of the Whinnies Brigade

Angelica

Daydream, wild moonflower horse. I am here. There is no need to worry now. I will keep you all safe: you, your two grown foals, Crystal and Rhythm, and your grand-foal, the one Crystal is carrying now, who is yet unborn.

Crystal. You look as if you are feeling well. Your foal is well, but you must relax, for her sake. Your nervousness affects her most of all. There is nothing to fear now. I will find the intruder and discover why the tampered grain was left with your dam last night. I am so grateful Daydream was suspicious. I am so glad she called me.

Rhythm, is your shoulder any better? No? It has been so long now, since your accident. I thought you would be well by now. I wish you did not have to feel this pain with every step, though I am grateful that most of the time, it is only a twinge and not unbearable. And I am glad your people see your value, even though you are still lame. Not all would. Your people must be special.

It is nice to see you all again so soon, in this paradise you call home: fields and forests, hidden meadows and clear, rushing streams. Sun and sighing winds. Warm rain. Beaches. All overlooked by this majestic volcano. Yet even in your beautiful home, danger has reared its poisoned head, like a serpent hidden in a garden.

1

We must dispose of the tampered grain so no other creature can find and consume it. We must let no harm fall to anyone or any thing. There is only one thing to do. We must bury the grain, deep in the earth. So deep it will not grow.

Come with me to the forest. No one will see us there. Daydream, tell me of the stranger as I dig a hole.

Come.

The gray car slowed as it drove past the driveway leading to Anela Ranch. The woman peered through the driver's window. Most of the house was hidden by vegetation and the woman couldn't see if Shelley's little red car was there or not. The monstrous dog shifted impatiently on the back seat behind her. A pathetic whine slid from his iron jaws.

"Be quiet! Quiet!" The words snapped through the interior of the car. The dog irritated the woman far more than she'd expected when she bought him the week before. Wolf was expensive, a trained attack dog, and she thought for all that money, she'd get a dog that didn't whine. She glanced over her shoulder and the dog trembled. He laid his wide head on his forepaws and rolled his eyes up to watch her. He whined again, a pathetic mewling noise. The woman ground her teeth in response.

She was well past the driveway now, but not past the property boundaries. Anela Ranch was huge. In fact, it was exactly 640 acres of forests, meadows, rocky shoreline and a beautiful black sand beach. A Hawaiian treasure. She knew how much of a treasure because it had been her home once, a long time ago.

Before Shelley's family stole it from her. She remembered every tree and stone of the vast meadows and forests. She remembered the darkest corners in the old house. She remembered every slat of wood and each nail in the sheds that now stood useless and decaying. She remembered everything. It made her angry to see how the place was falling apart. Shelley hadn't kept the ranch up at all.

But the woman planned to change that soon. After so many attempts, she had finally escaped the institution and now the time was right to set things straight. Thanks to her huge bank account, containing the hundreds of thousands of dollars from the settlement she'd won after her accident, she had more than enough money to pay a fair price.

I can't wait until its mine, she thought. Then everything will be all right again, I'll be happy, just like I was before Daddy was forced to sell. Like I was before the accident. And I'll never have to go back to that horrible, horrible place. She shuddered. The white walls, the nurses watching her every move, the bars on the windows, the psychologists analyzing her over and over and over; she couldn't bear to go back. And she didn't need to. There was nothing wrong with her. The doctors didn't know what they were talking about.

Her hands gripped the steering wheel harder and her knuckles turned white with tension. The only problem with the plan was that so far, Shelley had refused every single anonymous offer. I just have to make her sell. I have to offer her enough money or make her think the ranch is falling apart faster than it is, or make her think the stables are making her horses sick. And she'll sell. She has to. Has to.

4

"That ranch will be ours. Ours. Very soon." She squeezed the words through gritted teeth and slammed her fist down hard on the dashboard. *"Soon!"*

The woman jerked the car off the main road and onto an overgrown side road, refusing to slow down when the undercarriage of the car smacked into the ground. Saplings and branches scraped along the shiny new metal. The woman didn't care. It was a rental car. Let them repair the damage.

Out of sight of the main road, the woman slammed on the brakes and climbed out. When she opened the back door for the dog, he looked at her with questioning eyes.

"Get out!" she yelled. *"Are you stupid? Stupid? Do you have to wait for me to tell you everything to do?"* The dog was so irritating. Wasn't it obvious she wanted him to get out of the car? Why else would she open the door?

The dog leapt from the car and sat at her feet. She bent and tenderly stroked him on the head. Then she kicked him. The dog yelped in surprise and looked at her with frightened eyes, but he didn't move away. She smiled. Wolf would do what he was told.

"Good boy, Wolfie Wolf," she said, her voice sweet again, and the dog gazed up at her, relieved. *"Now let's go do what we came here to do."* She turned toward the trees and the dog slunk along by her side.

Just a little farther through the forest to the south pasture and they could begin their hunt for the horses.

Ali swung the empty bucket as she walked toward the feed shed. Halfway there, she spun in a circle, the bucket arching away from her body at arm's length. The medium-sized gray dog at her heels jumped back and cocked his head as he watched her.

"Sorry, Scruffy," Ali said, as she skipped on toward the shed. "I couldn't help it. I have the whole weekend without homework and that's something to celebrate! I wasn't trying to whack you on purpose. I just love Fridays." She ran the rest of the way to the shed. After the hustle and bustle of school and friends, activities and classes, it felt wonderful to get home and hang out with the horses and Scruffy. She felt so relaxed around the animals, totally and completely accepted. They weren't judging her or talking about her behind her back. Not like some of the kids at school.

It was strange, all the trouble she was having in school this year. Some of the more popular girls were being so mean to her, calling her "Horsey" behind her back and neighing when they wanted her attention. Not that Ali minded being called "Horsey". Of all the nicknames they could have chosen, she didn't mind that one too much. But they didn't mean it in a nice way at all.

Ali still hadn't figured out why they were acting differently this year. She had *always* loved horses, so why would they pick this year to start teasing her. Ali's best friend, Sarah, said it was because they were jealous. She was convinced it was because Ali was the prettiest girl in the class, yet at the same time, didn't even *try* to look good. She didn't wear the fancy clothes the popular girls wore or use makeup at all. Yet, according to Sarah, Ali, with her long dark hair, ivory skin and eyes so dark they almost looked black, was still prettier than all of them.

Most of the time Ali thought Sarah was being silly. Her best friend was always imagining some hidden plot or inventing intrigues. But now and then Ali wondered if she might be right. Some of the boys were treating her differently too, but in a nice way. A couple of the older boys even said "hi" when she passed them in the school hallway. It was a bit unnerving.

"But I don't need to worry about stupid 'human' stuff for the whole weekend," said Ali when she reached the shed. She knelt down and hugged Scruffy, then ruffled his ears. "Just dog and horse stuff, that's all. I'm part of the herd here and that's exactly the way I like it."

Ali opened the door to the dilapidated feed shed. Before stepping inside, she looked up. Nothing was poised to fall down on top of her. Last week an empty bucket had missed her by a hair and ever since then, Ali looked before she entered any of the old outbuildings on the ranch.

"All clear, Scruff," she said and patted the dog on his head. He looked up at her with adoring eyes. "Looks like you're doing a good job."

After the bucket had almost landed on her head, Ali finally clued in that all the strange things happening around the ranch weren't accidents. Someone was moving things, setting traps, trying to hurt her or the horses. Someone was invading their sanctuary.

At first Ali didn't know what to do. The only thing she knew for sure was that she couldn't tell her mother. Her mom was under too much pressure to sell the ranch as it was. She worked at a low paying job and could barely afford to keep the ranch, but that wasn't the only thing. Lately, big offers of money were coming in from someone who wanted to buy it. Then to top it off, everyone else seemed to think they should sell, even her mom's best friend, Maddie.

For a few seconds, Ali had considered confiding in Peter, her mom's boyfriend. She'd liked him before he started dating her mom. But in the end, she decided against it. She didn't want Peter to actually think she *approved* of him and her mom dating, because she didn't – at all! In fact, she would feel much better if the two of them decided to go back to being friends. Not that she hated Peter or anything. She just liked her family the way it was, with her and her mom, Scruffy, and the horses.

So instead of confiding in someone, she decided to take matters into her own hands. And Scruffy's paws. She started sneaking Scruffy outside to guard the property after her mom went to bed and letting him back inside before she got up in the morning. And so far Scruffy had kept the intruder away.

The first night he was outside, Scruffy barked at something. Ali was lying in bed, fully clothed, waiting for the alarm. When she hurried outside, she found him

8

standing in front of the stable door, staring off toward the distant trees and growling. But every night since had been uneventful. So much so that Ali had felt safe in letting Scruffy sleep at the foot of her bed again last night. She had missed his soft snores.

But that morning, in the early hours, Scruffy woke her with a heavy paw on her arm. She put him outside, still half asleep, then fell back into bed. Less than an hour later, Scruffy's barking woke her. With a groan, she climbed out of bed and staggered to the window. The gray dog was standing in the early dawn light, on guard outside the stable door. Ali threw on some clothes and crept quickly down the stairs but, once outside, she couldn't find anything amiss. Daydream was fine, wide awake in her stall and happy to see her. Ali spent most of the morning in the stable with the old mare and Scruffy. By the time the school bus arrived to pick her up, she had turned a well-groomed Daydream out to graze with the two younger horses, had a good breakfast, packed up her homework, and played with Scruffy for a while. It had been a great morning.

Ali walked to the only closed bin in the shed, the dog at her heels. She opened the bin and searched the shadows inside, in case something was left there. Something like the dead rabbit she'd found a couple weeks ago. But the bin held only grain. Ali's dark hair tumbled forward as she scooped the bucket full and lifted it out. She closed the grain bin tight before leaving the shed.

"Maybe the intruder is gone for good," she said to Scruffy as she walked toward the pasture, the full bucket swinging at her side. "I hope so. It's tense always wondering if Mom's going to find out." She climbed through the board fence, straightened and brushed the peeling paint from her sleeve. Her eyes wandered over the large pasture. Verdant green grass stretched out before her, growing thick and lush. Ancient forests edged the meadow and the volcano stood behind, stately and immoveable. Ali took a deep breath of the warm, perfumed air and allowed Anela Ranch to work its magic on her once again. The last bit of tension slowly trickled from her body.

"Let's check the south pasture first," she said to Scruffy when she didn't see the horses. She jogged toward the distant line of trees, the bucket banging against her leg and her feet swishing through the long grass. Scruffy trotted soundlessly beside her. When they reached the edge of the forest, they turned onto the trail that led to the south pasture. Ali slowed to a walk and Scruffy ranged around her, sniffing the ground.

The trail was soft underfoot. Ali looked up at the trees towering above her, huge giants waving their fronds in the warm breeze. The birds sang their evening song and the pure notes swirled around her. Too soon she broke into the south pasture. Her eyes searched the meadow. The sun was low on the horizon and shady fingers stretched from the far trees and sprawled across native grasses. The horses were still nowhere in sight.

"Where are they, Scruff? They wouldn't go all the way to the west pasture, would they? Not so close to suppertime. Maybe they're in the wildflower meadow," said Ali. She searched the ground. Fresh unshod hoof prints led to the left and Ali followed them along the edge of the forest.

A sudden clang of metal on rock made her stop short. She dropped to the ground, her heart in her throat. The bucket spewed grain across the grass but Ali hardly noticed. Quickly, she pulled Scruffy into her arms and clamped her hand over his muzzle so he wouldn't bark.

"Shhh. Quiet, boy," she whispered, in his ear. "Now, lie down. Good boy. Guard the oats," she commanded, her eyes attempting to penetrate the half-light beneath the trees. The clanging sound came again. And again. Ali felt a strange quiver run up her spine. Her breath quickened and she thought of turning Scruffy loose so he could chase the intruder away again. But this could be her only chance to find out *who* was sneaking around the ranch at night.

"Sorry, Scruffy. You've got to stay here. I can't take a chance that you'll bark," she whispered. "Someone's there in the woods, and I've got to see who it is. Now, stay."

Scruffy looked at her with eager eyes, his body trembling. Ali slowly released his muzzle and rose to her feet, then put her palm out flat toward him. "No, Scruffy. I mean it. Stay. Guard the oats. Stay." Scruffy whined when she turned away, but he didn't follow.

Quickly and silently, Ali ran toward a large tree at the edge of the forest and slipped into its deepest shadow. Slowly she leaned out from around the trunk and peered into the trees. She still couldn't see what was making the noise. She needed to go farther into the woods.

She flitted from tree shadow to tree shadow, deeper into the forest. It was getting dark beneath the trees. Twilight was swiftly coming on. Finally, she could see the horses, their rumps toward her. They were watching something or someone. Ali tried to see past them to whatever was holding their attention, but their

11

bodies were blocking her view. She darted to another tree and peeked out from around the trunk. Now only Crystal's rump was in the way, her hind socks glowing white in the shadows.

Halfway to the next tree, Ali stepped on a dry branch lying on the ground. The snap ricocheted through the air. She leapt for cover. Then, safely behind the tree, she held her breath and listened. There was no sound. No rustle of movement. Slowly, she leaned out from behind the tree trunk, just enough to see what was happening. All three horses were looking at her. Then Daydream nickered and walked toward her.

But Ali hardly saw the ancient mare. Her eyes were focused behind her, on a teenaged girl holding a shovel. A girl with long blonde hair that glimmered despite the gloom beneath the forest canopy. A girl with hazel eyes so light they glowed a luminous gold, and skin so pale she looked ghostly in the twilight.

"Hello." The melodious voice floated toward Ali like birdsong, like the wind dancing through the trees, as if it was a perfectly natural part of the forest. Of the land. As if this strange girl belonged at Anela Ranch, far more than Ali did.

Daydream walked to Ali and snuffled her shoulder with a greying muzzle. Ali's hand automatically slid along the old mare's rough neck, though her eyes didn't leave the strange girl.

"Do not be frightened," the girl said. She laid the shovel on the ground beside her. "I did not come to hurt the horses. I have come only to help them."

Ali was almost too afraid to breathe, let alone to speak. Was this the intruder? She didn't look mean. Only different, very, very different. "Who are you?" she asked in a tiny voice, her eyes locked onto the girl's golden ones.

"I am Angelica."

"Why are you here? What are you doing?"

"Come closer and I will show you."

Ali shook her head. There was no way she was coming closer, not until she figured out who this stranger was. Her fingers twisted in Daydream's long mane. The mare looked at her in the deepening twilight, then took a step toward the stranger. Ali jerked her hand away and Daydream stopped. She looked back at Ali with an inquisitive expression, as if to ask her why she wasn't coming.

"What have you done to Daydream?" Ali asked the girl, suddenly angry. No one had ever come between her and Daydream. Never. Until now.

"I am sorry," the girl said. "She did not mean to betray you. She is not afraid of me and is telling you there is no need for you to fear either."

"I don't believe you," accused Ali. "You've bewitched her or something."

"No, I am her friend."

"I want you to leave. Right now!"

Angelica looked down at the ground and scuffed the dirt with her foot. "I am sorry to have bothered you," she whispered. "I will leave soon. As soon as the horses are safe."

Ali felt a reluctant spark of sympathy. "What are you doing here?" she asked again, her voice a bit softer.

"I came to help the horses," Angelica said, looking up. Her face was hopeful. Anticipating Ali's question, she added, "I believe someone tried to harm Daydream last night. I came to help her and the others."

"What? Harm Daydream? Who tried to harm her?"

"I do not know. And Daydream cannot tell me. She did not know her."

"Her?" Ali had always assumed the intruder was a him. Daydream turned her head and snuffled Ali's hand with her muzzle.

"Come." Angelica's words were gentle. "I promise I will not hurt you. Your horses trust me. Do you not trust their judgement?"

Ali nodded her head and trailed her fingers from Daydream's star, down her dark face. Angelica was right. The horses did trust the strange girl. There was nothing but calmness and acceptance in Daydream's eyes. Crystal stood with one back leg resting and eyes half closed, while Rhythm sniffed at the shovel lying on the ground at Angelica's feet.

"Okay," Ali agreed. "I'll come closer. But only close enough to see what you're doing." Ali's insides fluttered as she took her first step toward Angelica and the crazy thought that she was changing her life by trusting the girl sprung into her mind.

I hope I'm doing the right thing, thought Ali, fighting her impulse to turn and run. Her breath came fast and shallow and she put her hand out and touched Daydream's neck. The old mare paced quietly beside her, lending her strength.

"I have buried the grain the woman left," said Angelica, motioning to the hole she was filling in when Ali stopped beside Crystal. An empty bucket lay beside the upturned earth. "It was left in the stable last night and, because the woman who left it acted so strange, Daydream was suspicious. She called me. I think the grain has been tampered with."

Ali was instantly speechless. A thousand questions galloped through her mind. What was so strange about the woman? And how could Daydream call Angelica? Was the girl walking past on the road and hear the mare neighing? No, Ali would have heard if Daydream had neighed that loud. But how else could Angelica know to come? And the grain might be tampered with? Was the woman trying to poison Daydream?

Why would anyone want to hurt her? Ali shuddered. She couldn't imagine what it would've been like to walk out to the stable that morning to find her beloved Daydream dead. Ali tore her mind from the gruesome image and tried to focus.

15

The intruder used to be happy just wrecking things around the ranch. Why is she suddenly trying to hurt the horses? What does she want? There's nothing she can gain from killing Daydream. Is there?

She had to find out who this woman, this intruder was. Ali looked at Angelica standing by the hole, patiently waiting for her to think things through. "You have to help us," she said, without stopping to think of the consequences of throwing her lot in with Angelica. "We've got to stop her before the horses get hurt."

Angelica nodded solemnly. "We will," she said. "Together."

"What is your name?" asked Angelica, in the silence that followed.

"Ali. And this is Daydream," Ali said. "The golden chestnut gelding is Rhythm and the red chestnut mare is Crystal."

Angelica smiled. "Yes, we have been introduced," she said and patted Crystal on the shoulder. The mare nickered to her, nuzzled her arm for a moment, and then turned to wander away. Rhythm followed her. "They want to graze a bit more before night comes," said Angelica.

"You understood what she said?" asked Ali, incredulously.

Angelica shrugged. "I understand horses. It is my gift and part of the reason I can help them. Though the sounds they make are not the only way they communicate. They also communicate through body language. They have other ways as well."

"Who are you, really?" Where are you from?" Ali asked, fighting to keep the suspicion out of her voice. Angelica seemed harmless and the horses liked her. *She can't be the intruder*, she reminded herself.

"I am… a traveler. I go to where horses are in trouble and I help them," Angelica said.

Ali crossed her arms over her midsection. "How do you know where to go?"

"I feel the horses' worry and fear. I am drawn to them. I do not know how but I appear where they are."

"So you're... " Ali stopped speaking. Angelica suddenly seemed larger than she had before. The golden hair and eyes were eerie in the twilight. Without thinking, she took a step back.

"Do not be afraid," said Angelica. "I have only come to help. I cannot hurt you or the horses, and I would not even if I could. My job is to help the horses and that means I will also help you and your companion, the dog who waits impatiently by the grain bucket you left him to guard. He did not guard the grain well, by the way. Crystal and Rhythm are eating it." She smiled.

"So you're... you're not human." The words squeaked from Ali's mouth.

"I have gifts that help me to help the horses. I can shift to different places and times in a heartbeat. I can communicate with horses. Other than that, I am like any other being. But that is not what is important, Ali. What *is* important is that someone wants to harm your horses. And we must stop her."

Ali nodded her head. She needed to clear her thoughts. Angelica was right. What mattered was the horses' safety. But she was sure Angelica was much less a "normal being" than she claimed. There was something very strange about the girl. *But she's strange in a good way,* Ali decided. *Hopefully, she has a lot of weird gifts; gifts we can use to find out who's been hanging around. We've got to find this woman before she hurts one of the horses.*

"You're right. What do we do now?" she asked.

18

"When Daydream told me of the intruder, there was something odd. Daydream did not know the woman, but still she found the woman familiar," said Angelica, picking up the shovel again.

"Familiar?" repeated Ali, and raised her eyebrows. "But if she didn't know her, how could she find her familiar?"

"I was hoping you would know," said Angelica and bent to shovel the rest of the dirt back into the hole.

"Daydream thought she seemed familiar," she repeated softly as she kicked some needles and leaves over the bare earth. How could Daydream find the intruder familiar, yet, at the same time, not know who she was? "Could she have smelled the intruder before? Like maybe on me or my mom's clothes? Or Peter's or Maddie's?" asked Ali, wracking her brain trying to think of anyone else who had been at Anela Ranch lately. "Or that real estate agent that came to visit. Daydream might have sniffed at her too."

"That could be it."

"Or could it be someone she knew a long, long time ago?" asked Ali.

"That could be it as well," said Angelica. "I have an idea. Maybe *you* will recognize the intruder. Daydream may be able to tell you about her."

Ali felt her heart quicken. "How?" she said in a small voice. This was sounding weird again, even scary.

"Stand in front of Daydream. It may help to touch her."

Ali moved close to the dark bay mare and leaned her head on Daydream's white star.

"Shut your eyes." Angelica paused for a few moments, then added, "Now ask Daydream about the

19

stranger, not in words, but in images. In impressions. Horses do not think in words or sentences or paragraphs. They think in full concepts: sight, smell, shape, feelings, sound, and more, all combined into a single complete image. They think of things as they *are*, not as they would be if they were interpreted into words. Do you understand what I mean?"

"I think so," said Ali, trying to concentrate. It was hard to not think in words. First she pictured the stable around her, the way she knew it felt at night, peaceful and silent. Then she concentrated on someone entering the stable. Finally she felt a question pull from the darkness behind her eyes, almost like an openness or empty space. It was human shaped, woman shaped. A blank outline for Daydream to fill in.

"Now let her tell you the answer." Angelica's voice seemed far away.

At first Ali saw nothing. Then she saw a wisp of dark, curly hair on the edge of the outline. It blurred again and there was nothing for a few moments.

Then Ali sensed a presence wend its way toward her. She reached out for it, eager to understand. Eager to see who the stranger was. But when the presence touched her, Ali recoiled. The hatred was so strong! But it wasn't directed toward the horses. No, the woman hated something else, *someone* else, with a passion that almost consumed her. And there was something else too, wasn't there? A faint niggling of something hiding beneath the hatred. Something important. Something Daydream wanted her to see.

But I can't look, she thought. *I just can't. What if it's something even worse than hatred?* She felt sick. Immediately she felt Daydream's presence comforting her, the old mare's warmth filling her. In Ali's mind, a soft white flower drifted down from above and silken petals brushed against her fingers.

An imaginary wild moonflower, Ali realized. *From Daydream, my magical moonflower horse. I've got to be strong, for her sake.*

She forced herself to mentally reach toward the presence again. She brushed it with tentative fingers of thought. The hatred pushed at her, tried to force her away, but Ali probed deeper. There *was* something else. Something almost feral. Unpredictable. Even twisted somehow. She gasped. Insanity! Could it be? Was the woman insane? Ali jerked away again.

But I still don't know who it is! Ali forced herself to stare into the shadow that was the creature's face, hoping it wouldn't step toward her. *Daydream's in control here,* she reminded herself. *She won't let anything happen to me.* Her eyes strained for a feature, any feature. Then she sensed it. A vague familiarity. Yes, she'd *seen* this person before. But the woman was different now. Very, very different.

Distant hoof beats, running fast.

Daydream jerked away from her. Ali's eyes sprung open. She staggered and almost fell to the forest floor. She shook her head, trying to scatter her dizziness. "What's wrong?" There was no answer.

Her vision cleared enough to see Daydream trot away through the trees, toward the south pasture. Angelica ran behind her. "What's wrong?" Ali yelled, loud enough for Angelica to hear.

"The horses!" Angelica yelled back over her shoulder. "We must hurry. Something is after the horses."

21

Daydream. Stay here in this meadow. Do not follow me along the trail to the main pasture. I must go alone.

I will save Rhythm and Crystal. Trust me. You must stay here and be safe. You must take care of Ali. Keep her away from this creature. He is consumed with bloodlust. I can sense it even from here. He has been frightened, traumatized, and he longs to feel powerful again, to triumph and conquer. He may even desire to kill.

Please stay!

The woman ran along the edge of the forest, trying to keep the racing horses and dog in sight. Wolf was doing a wonderful job. All of his aggression was being channelled into this chase. He was a leaping, growling fury. A slavering demon, his jaws snapping just inches from the gelding's back legs.

As she guessed he would, the gelding was keeping between the dog and the mare, protecting her. Totally unaware that all it would take is one rip, one tear, from Wolf's teeth to make him permanently lame in one of his back legs too. The horses galloped toward the trail to the larger pasture and disappeared through the trees, the dog right behind them.

The woman caught a movement out of the corner of her eye. A girl burst from the woods, her blonde hair glinting in the evening light.

The woman leapt behind the nearest tree and peered out from behind the trunk to watch the girl sprint after the horses. She could have sworn her enemy's daughter had dark hair, not blonde. Was she wrong? No, she couldn't be. Maybe it was a friend of the daughter's. But then, if she was a friend, what was she doing out here?

Moving swiftly, the woman hurried deeper into the forest, a dark shadow that hardly seemed to touch the ground. She didn't need the trail. She could cut through the woods.

Angelica

I must run faster. I must, somehow, stop the dog from attacking Rhythm, from causing Crystal to miscarry her unborn foal.

Oh no. Ali's dog! He runs to protect the horses and the black one attacks him!

How can I stop the black dog from tearing him apart? He is so much smaller than this intruder. He is a companion and a faithful friend, not a killer.

He will not stand a chance.

When the woman first heard the strange growling roar, she wasn't sure what it was. Then a dog yelped in pain. Wolf was fighting with Shelley's mutt. The black dog was already distracted from the horses.

She'd wanted to avoid killing any of the animals – unless she had to, of course. Chasing the horses and scaring them half to death was one thing. Even having Wolf bite the gelding was okay because he was lame anyway. But killing the dog?

She stopped under a large tree and leaned against the rough bark. On the other hand, with the dog gone it would be easier to roam about the ranch at night again. She could set more traps for Shelley and her brat. Not that she'd have to, but it was only fair. Why should only the animals suffer? Her enemy deserved worse than her horse being sick and her dog killed. She deserved to be hurt too.

The dog's cries grew louder, more desperate. Echoing pain. The woman put her hand to her mouth. Such anguish in those cries. Such agony!

Should she do it? Should she allow Wolf to kill Shelley's dog?

Ali ran as fast as she could behind Daydream and Angelica, but they were much faster. By the time she reached the edge of the trees, Angelica was gone. Ali stopped beside Daydream.

"Which way did they go, girl?" she asked. Daydream nickered to her. "And where's Scruffy?" Her eyes swept over the pasture, but the gray dog was nowhere in sight. Ali ran to the empty bucket. "We've got to find them," she said to Daydream. The bay mare nickered again. "They must have run back toward the house. Come on!"

Daydream whinnied again, louder this time and Ali turned back. The mare wasn't following her. "What's wrong, girl?" Ali crooned as she walked back to the old mare. "I can't leave you here all by yourself." She slipped off her jacket and threw one sleeve around Daydream's neck. "Come on, girl. Let's go find the others." She pulled on the makeshift rope and Daydream reluctantly stepped after her.

They were halfway along the trail leading to the big pasture in front of the house, when Ali heard the first distant yelp. She stopped in her tracks and strained to hear. From far away, she heard a strange growling rumble. It took her a moment to realize the sound was fighting dogs. Scruffy had attacked whatever was chasing the horses.

"Stay here, Daydream!" she yelled and ran toward the pasture. She saw them the second she broke from the path through the trees, Scruffy and a big black dog locked together in battle about halfway to the house. Behind them, Rhythm and Crystal pressed against the fence, eager to escape. Angelica ran toward the fighting canines.

Ali felt her heart was going to stop when the black dog pushed Scruffy over backward and leapt on top of him. Fangs flashed at the gray dog's throat and face. Scruffy met the dog with open jaws and sharp teeth but, even from a distance, Ali could see the other dog was much bigger and stronger. And he looked like he'd been bred to fight.

Ali raced toward the two dogs. Scruffy's cries punctuated the larger dog's snarls again and again. Ali pumped her arms and legs harder, harder, trying to run faster, trying to reach Scruffy before it was too late. She had to save him! She had to help Angelica! The golden girl was almost to where the two twisted together in a black, gray and red mass. With every second, the red color spread. Blood. Scruffy's blood.

Ali stumbled to a quick stop when a flash of light arched from Angelica's hands, instantly surrounding the two struggling dogs in a glowing mist. The black dog looked up in surprise. It was all Scruffy needed. He squirmed from under his attacker and dragged himself toward Angelica. Ali watched in awe as Angelica stepped between Scruffy and the ferocious killer. She was so brave! Light sparked across her hair and arms as if electrical currents were skimming over her body. The bright mist around the dog fell away and he snarled and stepped forward, his eyes locked on Angelica.

He's going to attack her anyway, realized Ali. *I've got to help her and Scruffy.* She darted forward again, yelling as loud as she could and waving her arms. Scruffy somehow got three of his four legs beneath him and turned to face the black brute. A growl burst from his bleeding jaws. Angelica sent another series of sparks toward the dog. And finally he turned away.

"The horses!" shrieked Ali. Now the black dog was trotting toward Crystal and Rhythm. "He's going after the horses again!"

Angelica took only a couple steps toward the dog, when a high-pitched whistle burst from the forest. Instantly, the dog dropped to his belly, his ears flat against his skull. Ali was shocked. This was the ferocious killer from just moments before? A whine slid from the dog's throat and he crawled a few more inches toward the horses. He froze when the whistle came again and, after a moment's hesitation, slunk toward the trees, his head down and tail between his legs. Within seconds, he disappeared into the dark forest.

Ali ran the last few steps to Angelica and Scruffy. "Oh no, poor Scruffy," she whispered and dropped to her knees beside her beloved dog. He was covered with blood and, now that the black dog had gone, had collapsed to the ground.

With a quick intake of breath, Ali looked back toward the south pasture. Night was quickly coming on. "Where's Daydream?" she asked. A sudden vision of the black dog skulking off through the night to find the old mare startled her.

"Do not worry," said Angelica, bending over Scruffy. "She has joined the others at the fence."

Ali felt an explosion of relief. At least Daydream, Crystal, and Rhythm were okay. But Scruffy was seriously injured. "We've got to take him to the vet. Mom should be home from work soon. When she gets here, we can take him. If the clinic's still open."

"I will help you carry him to the house," offered Angelica. "We can keep him warm there, until your mother comes. Then I will follow the black dog to see where he goes."

"Do you think he'll lead you to where he lives?"

"He did not come here on his own. His handler was there, in the woods, watching. She is the one who whistled to him, calling him back to her. I am sure she is the one who left the grain. She wants to hurt or kill the horses and this time, she sent the dog to attack them."

"But why?" Tears choked Ali's voice. "I still don't understand. Why would someone want to hurt some innocent horses and a harmless old dog?"

Angelica put her hand on Ali's shoulder. "We will find out, Ali," she said. "I promise. But later. Now we will care for brave Scruffy."

They moved Scruffy as gently as possible, but even then, he whined and whimpered with every step they took. It took fifteen minutes to carry him to the house. Carefully, they laid him on a thick quilt in front of an electric heater and turned the heater on high. Ali tucked part of the quilt around him.

"What if the dog comes back while we're at the vet?" asked Ali, her voice trembling. Now that they had Scruffy safe in the house, she found her hands were shaking too.

"I can stay with the horses. Do not worry. I will keep them safe," said Angelica.

Ali relaxed. If anyone could keep the horses safe, it would be Angelica with her magical powers. "Should we put them in the stable?" she asked. "That way if the dog comes back, he can't get them."

"That would keep them safe from the dog, but not from his mistress, especially now that Scruffy is not here to guard them," replied Angelica. "I do not like the thought of them being locked in an enclosed space at night. It may be better if they are all in one of the distant pastures. Then they can run if someone approaches them. I will stay with them as much as I can, and if I have to go to another, I will make sure no one is near before I leave."

"Thanks Angelica." Ali rubbed Scruffy gently on his head. She drew a deep breath. "You forgot to tell me you could create light when you were explaining how you're different from humans," she said. "But thanks for doing that. For saving Scruffy."

"You helped save him too, you know," said Angelica. "My light was not enough. If you had not run toward us, yelling, the dog may have attacked again."

"It was good we were both there. And as long as Scruffy's okay, it was good he was there too. Otherwise the dog would've attacked the horses. But if Scruffy's not okay... " Ali bit her lip. She couldn't finish the sentence.

31

"Try not to worry, Ali." Angelica's hand was gentle on her shoulder. "Just be as strong as you can. That is the best way you can help Scruffy right now. If you are frightened, he will be too."

Ali nodded. "I'll try," she whispered and looked up at the older girl. For the first time she noticed Angelica looked a little pale. She didn't have the same energy about her that she had before the dog attacked, before she'd saved Scruffy by flashing her light. "Are you okay?" she asked.

Angelica nodded. "I am a little tired, that is all."

"I wish Mom would hurry."

As if on cue, Ali saw lights flash against the wall. Her mom was home from work, driving her little car into the driveway.

"I must go," said Angelica. "I must find the dog before he goes too far. I will talk to you tomorrow morning and tell you what I discover tonight." She hurried to the door and opened it but, just before she slipped through, she turned back to Ali. "Do not tell your mother about me, Ali. It will only complicate things further."

"I won't. I don't think she'd believe me anyway and, besides, she has enough to worry about."

Angelica smiled and disappeared through the front door, shutting it at the same moment Ali's mother opened the door from the garage.

"Mom!" Ali called, tears catching at her voice. "Come quick! Scruffy's been hurt!"

Angelica

It is too dark to track him. I can only follow his life force, the residue of his energy as it winds back through the trees.

And while I am gone, you, my dears, must go to one of the distant meadows. Try to find someplace high so you can see all around you, and watch for any who may come near. Plan an escape route so you can run if you must. When I am finished here, I will come to you. I will stay with you this night. I will keep you safe.

But before you go, I thank you for restoring my energy with your tears, Daydream. Words are not enough to thank you. I will see you soon.

The dog's energy is strong here at the edge of the forest; his bloodlust is like a living creature raging in the shadows. Yet he is submissive to his mistress and he obeys her, at least for now. But he went to her reluctantly. Very reluctantly.

The dog is deadly, yes. But the truly dangerous one is his mistress, the one who uses and controls him. She is the one to fear, the one who will strike again, if not with the dog, then in a new way. She is the one I must find.

I am too late. His trail leads to a side road off the highway. This is where she rewarded him and here is where he got into her car and they drove away. Their energy is still very strong in this place, but I will not catch them this time.

The woman drove back past Anela Ranch without glancing down the driveway. There was no point. Shelley wouldn't have the dog in the car yet. But it wouldn't be long and she could pay the ranch another visit. All she had to do was drive a short distance down the road, park and wait for her enemy to pass her on their way to the vet, and then drive back to the ranch.

The woman sighed. She knew she had no choice now but to change her tactics. She finally realized that her sabotage and harmless traps would never make Shelley sell the ranch. There was only one way to make her leave. She had to bring real tragedy into her enemy's life. Not that she minded giving Shelley something to cry about. She just hated to see the animals suffer.

But they're suffering anyway, she rationalized. That dark horse is so old, it must be in tremendous pain, all the time. And the gelding is lame. He suffers with every step he takes.

As soon as she'd seen the old horse join the others at the fence, she'd known what she had to do. In a way, the old one deserved to be the first target. It should have eaten the grain she'd taken the trouble to prepare. Yes, tonight she would send Wolf after the old horse.

The effect would be quite dramatic: Shelley finding the horse ripped to shreds. The woman ran her hand through her dark curls. She felt a little sorry for the old thing – it would have a horrible death. She hoped it wouldn't scream. She didn't know what she'd do then. She wouldn't want to stop Wolf but it would sound so awful. Maybe if she plugged her ears. And told herself over and over that she was really helping the horse. Putting it out of its misery. Doing it a favour.

"Favour," she whispered. "Favour. Favour."

For a moment she considered the other two horses. The young mare was a beautiful animal, shiny and bright. There was nothing wrong with her at all.

I can buy her with the ranch, the woman thought, pleased. She'll have such pretty babies too, and I can keep all of them. She smiled. She could just picture herself sitting on the patio with her feet up, Wolf lying beside her, and the gleaming chestnut mare grazing in the pasture, a strong healthy foal leaping and playing around her.

She tried to picture the lame horse being there, but couldn't. No, it would have to go. There was no room for a defective horse in her pasture. It would be her second target if killing the old mare didn't make Shelley sell. It felt good to have a backup plan.

"A favour," she whispered again. "Favour." She giggled.

On the seat behind her, Wolf whined.

"He was beaten up by another dog," Ali said in a high, thin voice when her mom hurried into the room.

A quick intake of breath and Ali's mom was kneeling at Scruffy's side, her white-blonde hair almost brushing the bloody side. "What happened? Whose dog?"

"I don't know. He was after the horses and Scruffy stopped him by attacking. But the other dog was bigger and a lot meaner," said Ali, fighting back tears. "Scruffy's going to be okay, isn't he, Mom?"

Shelley didn't answer her question. "What about you, Ali? Are you okay?" she asked, her piercing blue eyes on her daughter's face. "Did the dog hurt you at all?" When Ali shook her head, she continued. "I'll phone the vet and see if we can get Scruffy in right away." She hurried to the telephone.

"But they'll be closed," said Ali. "Isn't it too late?"

"They open up the clinic for emergencies. It costs a lot, but – oh, hello, Doctor Blake. This is Shelley Taylor. No, no it's not Daydream. It's Scruffy. He's been in a fight. Can we bring him in right away? He looks pretty bad."

Ali stroked Scruffy's forehead as her mom made arrangements. "It's okay, Scruff," she murmured. "Just hold on. Hold on, buddy."

Then her mom was off the phone and it was time to move Scruffy out to the car. Instead of picking him up this time, they each grabbed two corners of the folded quilt and, keeping the blanket taut so Scruffy could lie flat in the middle, they carried him out to the car. They slid him as gently as they could onto the back seat, got into the car and pulled slowly out of the garage. Even though they were only creeping along, Ali heard Scruffy whimpering in the back seat.

"Oh no, I forgot. Peter is coming over for dinner tonight. I'll be back in a minute," said Ali's mom, letting the car roll to a careful stop. When she ran back into the house, Ali slipped from the front seat. Scruffy sprawled across most of the back seat, but if she sat right against the door, there was enough room for her to sit without bumping him. She shut the door behind her, then rubbed Scruffy on his forehead. His tongue slipped out of his mouth and tried to reach her hand.

"It's okay, buddy," said Ali. "Don't move." She put her hand down by his mouth and his pink tongue reached out and licked her fingers. "I should be saying thanks, Scruffy. Not you," she added and reached for the top of his head again. "Thanks so much for saving the horses. And don't worry. You're going to be okay. You've got to be." She turned her head and impatiently watched the house. Her mom hurried out the front door and tacked a note to it, then ran to the car.

"Okay, let's go," she said as she slipped behind the wheel. "The vet will be there soon."

When the dilapidated red car passed her, the woman turned the headlights on, drove her car off the side road and headed back to Anela Ranch. She guessed she had an hour at least, and probably longer.

She'd been thinking while she waited and had the entire evening planned out. First she would make sure Wolf killed the older horse, somewhere close to the house so Shelley would find the carcass that night. Then she'd go into the house.

She could leave a message for her enemy there. One she wouldn't miss – "YOU'RE NEXT" scrawled in her own lipstick across her bathroom mirror. That would scare her half to death. She knew she wouldn't have to do much more. Shelley was a coward. Just frightening her could be enough.

The woman happily drummed her stubby fingernails on the steering wheel. There was only one thing wrong with the plan: she wouldn't be there to see the first tears of grief or hear the heartbroken sobs. She wouldn't see the glimmer of curiosity on Shelley's face when she first saw the writing. She wouldn't see the sheer terror after the words were read. How she would dearly love to see that!

Well, maybe she could. There was a closet in the room. If the door was opened a crack, she might witness the flood of tears, the delightful weakness, the fear and hysteria, the panicky phone calls.

Yes, she would wait in the closet. Watch and revel in her brilliant plan.

Angelica

Daydream, Rhythm, Crystal. What a perfect place you have chosen to hide. This little clearing backed against the cliffs, where none can attack you from behind. It is higher than the rest of the land and will give a good view of anyone approaching, plus there is plenty of grass for one night and a stream tumbles down the cliff behind you to pool near your hooves.

But most important of all, it is far from the house and stable. You should be safe here as long as the dog does not track you. I will scout out the forest and the trail leading to this haven, just in case.

And you, you should rest, my dear ones. We do not know what tomorrow will bring, but whatever it is, we want to be ready.

The gray car lurched into the driveway and bumped over the potholes toward the house. As the woman had expected, Anela Ranch was deserted. She parked the car so the headlights would shine into the pasture.

"Looks like we'll have to do a bit of horse hunting first. Yes, hunting. Hunting," she murmured when she didn't see the horses' eyes glowing in the car's lights. "Unless they're in the stable. We'll check there first. Yes, first check there."

The dog whined in response. The woman laughed and reached over the seat. She smacked him sharply on the head. Not that she cared that he whined right then. In fact, sometimes she even liked it. Wolf was a terrifying beast, yet he was always reminding her of how powerful she was. How invincible and strong. She wondered, not for the first time, why he was so frightened of her. It's not like she would ever hurt him, not really hurt him.

She turned off the headlights and opened the car door, then walked around to the trunk to get the flashlight. It was under the bloody towels she'd wiped Wolf with after his fight. Not his blood, the other dog's blood. Wolf hardly had a mark on him. She closed the trunk with a bang and reached to open the back door and let the dog out.

A light flashed across the house and she released the door handle and spun around. It was too late to hide. Someone was pulling into the driveway and the vehicle lights were swinging toward her. The woman opened the door to the front seat and slipped behind the wheel, closing and locking the door behind her just in time to avoid the lights. Her breath came sharp and quick. How could they be back already? Had the dog died? Or had her enemy forgotten something?

The vehicle stopped behind hers and the lights extinguished. The dog growled.

"Shut up!" The whispered command slashed through the air. "Lie down. Down." She felt the car move as the dog settled reluctantly on the seat.

A dark shape loomed toward her. "Hello?" A man's voice.

The woman unrolled the window a crack. "Hi. Sorry. Sorry. I was just leaving," she said, in what she hoped was a nice voice. "No one seems to be home."

"That's odd," said the man. "I know Shelley and Ali planned on being home tonight. I wonder if anything's wrong."

"Their dog was hurt," she offered. "They took it to the vet. Vet."

"Oh no!" The man leaned forward to look in her window. "Poor Scruffy. What happened?"

"I don't know." The woman shrank away from his gaze. Too late she realized telling him she knew about the dog was a mistake. She started the car. "I've got to go. Go. Move your car. I've got to go. I've got to. Go."

The words fell over each other in a tumble. The dog picked up the panic in her voice and growled quietly.

The man stepped back, surprised. Then he leaned forward again. She could sense his suspicion as he peered into the dark interior. "Can I tell Shelley who dropped by? I know she'll hate having missed you, Miss... uh... "

"Just a friend. Just a friend." The woman started to roll up the window.

"Maddie?" His voice was surprised. "I thought your voice sounded familiar. Is everything okay? You sound upset."

The woman didn't bother replying. How could she be so dumb? She'd let him too close and now he thought he knew her. She ought to make Wolf bite her. A punishment for being so stupid.

"I shouldn't have said anything, anything," she whispered when the window was closed.

She jammed the car into reverse and waited impatiently, staring away from the man and tapping her black painted fingernails on the steering wheel. Finally, he took the hint and walked back to his truck. He drove it to the side so she could back out the driveway.

She turned onto the main road, put the car into gear and shoved the accelerator to the floor. The tires squealed as she sped away. She slammed her hand against the steering wheel and screamed in frustration. The dog whimpered on the back seat.

"Shut up!" she shrieked at him. "Don't you ever shut up? Shut up? Can't you let me think?" They rounded a sharp turn in the road and the ocean stretched along beside them. The moon was slowly rising above the *distant horizon and the beach glistened below, the black sand glowing silver in the moonlight. Low tide.*

The woman smiled and pressed on the brake. She knew what she could do. It was a long shot, but she just might get Shelley after all. Maybe a bit of sabotage was still in order.

Ali

Shelley took the corners as carefully as she could and slowed down for all the bumps and potholes in the road. It seemed to take forever to reach the veterinary clinic. They arrived just as Doctor Blake was pulling into the driveway in his beat-up pickup. Ali's mom parked the car and jumped out to greet him.

Ali watched them talk for a moment through the car window. When they walked into the clinic, she looked down at Scruffy. He was staring at her, his eyes large and trusting. Ali felt her tears well up again. Had this happened to Scruffy because she hadn't said anything to her mom about the strange things that were happening around the ranch? Would the intruder have had the chance to bring the poisoned grain or the killer dog onto the property if *both* Ali and her mother were watching?

"Should I tell her, Scruff? Should I tell her what's been going on?" Gently she stroked the dog's head. The smell of blood was strong in the car. She wished her mom and the vet would hurry.

Another vehicle pulled into the clinic parking lot and Ali looked up. It was Peter. Ali watched his tall, gangly form hurry to the car. "How is he, Ali?" he said, after opening the door. The concern in his voice almost made Ali soften toward him. Almost.

"He'll be fine," said Ali, staring down at Scruffy.

"Of course he will." Peter's voice was gentle and Ali looked up at him with hopeful eyes. If only it were true. It had to be true. She couldn't bear it if it weren't.

Just then her mom and Doctor Blake walked out of the clinic. The veterinarian had a stretcher under his arm. Ali rubbed Scruffy's head as Doctor Blake positioned the stretcher, then moved aside so Peter and Shelley could pull Scruffy and the quilt onto the stretcher. Peter grabbed the opposite end of the stretcher and he and Doctor Blake carried Scruffy to the clinic. Ali's mom held the door open and Ali followed them through the cheerful waiting room and into one of the examination rooms. When they laid Scruffy on the examination table, she moved to his side and continued to stroke his head. She heard the front door to the clinic open and a few seconds later, the vet's assistant bustled into the room.

Doctor Blake glanced up at Ali's mom. "Shelley, this is going to take at least an hour. You're welcome to wait here, but it may make time pass more quickly if you go for a coffee or something."

"Good idea," said Peter. "We can go for a quick bite to eat and be back within the hour."

"But he's going to be okay, isn't he, Doctor?" Ali couldn't stop the words from popping out of her mouth.

"I haven't done my examination yet, Ali. Let's just say that, at this point, it looks promising, okay?"

"Thanks, Doctor," said Shelley. She put her arm around Ali's shoulder.

Ali leaned down and kissed Scruffy on the forehead. "You better be okay, Scruff," she whispered. "And don't worry. Doctor Blake is nice. I'll see you in an hour." Her mom led her away.

Outside the vet clinic, Ali took a deep trembling breath. One long hour. They had to wait for one hour. Just two TV sitcoms. One class at school. She could do that, though she knew it would be the longest hour of her life.

She was right. Ali hardly tasted the food her mother ordered for her. She didn't even try to smile at Peter's attempts to lighten her worry. She was relieved when he finally gave up and turned his attention back to Shelley. As the adults talked, Ali played with her food, pushing it to one side of her plate, then the other. The hum of conversation in the restaurant blended into the background. Ali was mashing each individual french fry into pulp with her fork when she heard her mom ask if Peter had trouble finding the note on the door.

There was a moment of silence, then "What note?"

"I left a note on the door saying we were at the veterinary clinic," explained Ali's mom.

"You didn't read it?" Ali asked, looking up from her mutilated food.

"No. Maddie was there. She told me."

"That's odd. I wasn't expecting Maddie to drop by tonight," said Shelley.

"She seemed upset you weren't there," said Peter.

"She was probably upset about Scruffy after reading the note," suggested Ali's mom.

"Maybe," said Peter, his words coming slowly. "But it seemed more than that. She seemed, well, strange. She wasn't acting like herself. And, come to think of it, there was another weird thing."

A chill ran down Ali's spine. "What?" she asked.

48

"I don't think she had time to read the note. I saw her turn into your driveway when I came around the last corner and, when I parked behind her, she was inside the car. There's no way she would've had time to walk up the front door, read the note and walk back to the car. And she wasn't in her usual car. She normally drives that little blue bug, doesn't she?"

Both Ali and her mom nodded.

"Then it definitely wasn't her car, unless she just bought a new one." He took another bite of supper, oblivious to the alarm in Ali's eyes.

Ali tried to steady her voice. "It must have been someone else," she suggested casually.

Peter chewed his mouthful thoughtfully and Ali wanted to reach out and pull the words from his mouth. "No, I'm sure it was her," he finally said.

"It was dark though," said Ali's mom. She took another bite of her dinner.

Ali blocked out their voices again and speared the last of her soggy french fries. If the person in the car hadn't had time to read the note, there was only one way she would know Ali and her mom had taken Scruffy to the vet. She was the owner of the attack dog.

But it couldn't be Maddie. Maddie and her mom had been best friends since kindergarten. Maddie would never harm them. Would she?

The woman lowered herself carefully down the steep trail her father had built years before, the dog fluid in the moonlight behind her. Climbing down the well-made trail, she allowed her respect and admiration for her father to come to the surface. He'd tried so hard to make money from the ranch before he'd been forced to sell it.

The most successful attempt was the trail, the public access he built to the beach on the ranch, known to be one of the most beautiful beaches on the island. But in the end, it still hadn't been enough. He had to borrow money from Shelley's dad to pay his gambling debts, but when he hadn't been able to pay back all his loans, they'd lost the ranch. And then, the accident. The most horrible day of her life.

With firm and practiced resolve, the woman pushed the experience out of her mind. There were other things to think about now. She'd spent too many years, going over and over and over the events of that day, millions of conversations with millions of doctors. There was nothing left to even think about.

The woman pushed the bushes aside and her feet followed the familiar trail as if she had traveled it yesterday. Still, she was grateful the moon was out. Without it, she wouldn't have found her way so easily. The flashlight she carried from the car was useless. The batteries were almost dead and the light dimmed not far from the car. She flung it into the bushes and, when the dog bounded after it, she yelled at him. He slunk back to her, a black, quivering hulk, then followed her meekly as she climbed down, down, down to the beach.

Finally she stepped onto the black sand. The dog ranged around her and loped to the edge of the rustling waves. He trotted along the waterline, his head down, sniffing at seaweed and other flotsam.

The woman didn't mind. It was a good place for him to get some exercise and the tide would wash away his paw prints. She walked purposefully along the beach, her head high, looking for the little boat that used to be there. There it was: a black lump hunkered above the high tide line. She chuckled and her fingers brushed against the twisted iron of the drill in her pocket.

"Ali, didn't you hear me?"

Ali looked up. "Sorry, Mom. I was just thinking."

"I asked you what happened to Scruffy. You said he was attacked by a big dog and it was chasing the horses?"

Ali nodded. "It was after Crystal and Rhythm. Daydream was with me. And Scruffy jumped between them. He saved them."

"Have you seen it around before?"

"No, never."

"Did you see any strangers around? Anyone it could have belonged to?" asked Peter.

"No." Ali shook her head.

"I wonder if we should file a report at the police station," said Ali's mom. She looked at Peter. "What if it comes back and attacks the horses again? Or worse, what if it attacks Ali!" She turned back to her daughter and Ali could see the fear in her eyes. "Did it act aggressively toward you?"

For a second, Ali hesitated. She didn't want to lie. But she didn't like it when her mom worried too much either. *And he didn't actually threaten me,* she reasoned. *He wanted to attack Angelica for a second, but not me.* She shook her head. "No," she added for emphasis. "It ran away when I got close." *And that's true,* she thought. *His owner just called him first.*

"We'll go to the police station in the morning. If we're lucky, they'll know whose dog it is." She turned back to Peter and her voice became hard. "People should be more careful with their pets, especially if they're dangerous. A dog like that should be tied up all the time. I can't believe someone was just letting it run loose. It could have easily attacked... "

"Can we go back to the clinic now?" Ali asked in an effort to stop her mother's rant before she gathered steam. She couldn't bear the thought of Scruffy lying still and bloody any longer, not without being nearby. Even if they had to sit in the waiting room, she wanted to be close to him.

"Sure, honey," said Ali's mom, her voice softening. "We'll go right away."

As one, they rose from the table. Peter stopped to pay for the meal while Ali and her mom waited. Ali's mom put her hand on her daughter's shoulder. "Don't worry so much, sweetheart," she said gently. "Scruffy will be fine. And the police will find who the dog belongs to. They have ways of finding these things out."

"I'm okay, Mom," said Ali in a small voice. "Really."

If only she could tell her mother how much more complicated everything was than an unleashed dog attacking the horses. But she couldn't. It could be the final straw to make her mom sell the ranch. Especially if she knew her daughter was in danger. No, Ali had to bear the burden alone.

Not alone, she suddenly remembered, and a wave of pure relief washed through her body. *Angelica can help me. And she's a great person to have on my side.*

Despite being gone for dinner, they sat in the waiting room for almost another hour. The clock on the walk dragged on and on, drawing every second into at least five. Ali listened to the murmur of voices behind the door as Doctor Blake and his assistant worked on Scruffy. She was sure the murmurs sounded worried and wrung her hands, twisting her fingers around each other until they were sore. Finally she couldn't stand anymore. She jumped up from her chair and began to pace the waiting room.

"What's taking them so long?" she asked, even though she knew her mom wouldn't be able to answer her. Just then the door between the two rooms opened. Ali rushed toward Doctor Blake. "Is he okay? Is Scruffy okay?"

Doctor Blake smiled. "Yes, he'll be fine, Ali. He had a lot of cuts that needed stitching, a broken leg that needed setting, and he lost a lot of blood. But with the good care I know you'll give him, he'll get better."

Ali felt as if she was going to collapse with relief. She felt her mom's hand on her shoulder and turned to hug her. "Can she see him?" she heard her mom ask the veterinarian. Ali pulled away to look at Doctor Blake and gave him her most beseeching, wide-eyed look.

"Not right now. He's still under the anaesthetic. It'll be a while yet, and then he's going to be groggy. You'll have to leave him here tonight. The soonest I can let him go home is tomorrow morning. And that's if he's responding well."

"But he'll miss us," protested Ali.

"Don't worry Ali. He's resting peacefully right now and that's the best thing for him," said Doctor Blake. "Rest. He'll take hours to completely wake up."

"We'll be here by eight then, Doctor," said Ali's mom. "And thanks for everything you've done."

"Yeah, *thanks*," said Ali. She'd never meant a "thanks" more in her life and hoped that Doctor Blake could tell how grateful she was.

Once outside the clinic, Peter took Ali's mom's hand in his. "Are you still into watching a video?" he asked. "If you're too tired after all this, it's okay."

"No, I'm fine. Actually it'll be nice to sit down and forget about our worries for a while, won't it, Ali?"

"Right," Ali said, grudgingly. The last thing she wanted to do was watch a video with Peter and her mom, but she supposed she owed Peter something after he'd been so worried about Scruffy.

Ali and her mother climbed into their car and drove out of the parking lot. As they left the veterinary clinic, Peter's truck pulled out behind them.

"I'm really tired, Mom," said Ali. "I think I'll go upstairs and read instead of watching the video. Do you mind?"

"Are you sure you're okay, honey?" The worry was creeping back into her mother's voice, now that they were alone together.

"Yeah, I'm fine. Just tired." The quiet noise of the tires on the road hummed through the car and Ali watched the black ribbon of asphalt unwind before them. "This is going to cost a lot, isn't it?" she asked.

"We'll use the horse money to pay for it," said her mom.

"But what if there isn't enough to last the horses the whole year? We can't sell them. You know what would happen to Daydream and Rhythm." Her voice was high and tight.

Her mom reached out and touched Ali's knee. "Don't worry so much, Ali. That's my job. I'll take care of everything. Just don't worry."

But Ali couldn't stop from worrying. She knew the only way they could afford to keep the horses was with the money they made every year from the sale of Crystal's foal. The money was put into a separate bank account and used to buy feed and grain for Daydream, Rhythm and Crystal, as well as the farrier costs, their shots, and the stud fee and expenses for the foal Crystal would have the following year.

It always broke Ali's heart to sell the beautiful weanlings. Every year she watched Crystal's baby walk into the horse trailer belonging to the new owner and be driven away. Two of the foals she'd never seen again. But they had to do it. There was no other way to keep the three horses they had.

"Ali, you're worrying. I can feel it," her mom said.

Ali sighed. If her mother only knew how much there was to worry about.

Her mom turned the car into the driveway. Ali exhaled when the house came into view. It felt *so* good to be home. Even though someone might have been

56

skulking around while they were gone. No not someone. Maddie. Peter said it was Maddie. *But I don't believe it,* Ali decided. *Maddie would never hurt any of us. Peter's wrong.*

When her mom stopped the car, Ali jumped out. "I'll be inside in just a minute, Mom," she said. "I want to see if the horses are nearby."

"Sure, honey," said Ali's mom.

Ali walked toward the pasture. The white peeling fence glowed in the moonlight. She heard Shelley greet Peter and the two of them go inside the house, their voices soft in the night. Then the door closed behind them.

Ali climbed up on the board fence and searched the moonlit pasture. The horses were gone. With a sigh she climbed down and walked toward the house. She would just have to trust that Angelica had them somewhere safe.

Angelica

Dawn trickles into the sky. The birds awaken. The night's vigil is over and we are safe. We thank you, Great One. We thank you for the morning, so pure and sweet. We thank you for the reawakening of the world, for the light that overtakes the darkness once again. We thank you for a new day reborn.

Ali stretched with her eyes closed and arms above her head. A small smile slid over her lips. It was Saturday. No school until Monday!

"Scruffy," she whispered. No snoring. No sound of toenails on the floor. No panting. Ali sat up in bed. "Scruffy?" Then she remembered. Scruffy was at the animal hospital. She looked at the digital clock by her bedside. Six o'clock. Ali groaned and threw herself back on her pillow. "Why did I wake up so early?" she complained, then pulled the quilt over her head. "That sucks. Two hours to wait."

She heard a faint whinny through the muffling of the pillow. "Daydream?" Ali threw the blankets aside and jumped out of bed. She raced to the window. The three horses were at the fence. And someone was on Rhythm's back. Angelica. Ali blinked, then rubbed her eyes. She wasn't dreaming. Angelica's hair *was* the same color as Rhythm. Chestnut locks spilled over the girl's shoulders and brushed across Rhythm's back. "Another thing she didn't tell me," Ali noted dryly.

Angelica leaned forward and whispered in Rhythm's ear. The gelding nickered and leapt forward into a gallop. Ali smiled as the gelding raced across the meadow, his sister close behind him. Rhythm's lameness wasn't too bad today. It was odd how some days were worse than others for him. The two horses galloped in a large circle, then joined their dam again at the fence. When Angelica looked toward the house, Ali waved through the window. Angelica waved back and slid from Rhythm's back.

Within a couple minutes, Ali was dressed and down the stairs. She ran out the back door, toward the pasture. "You kept them safe," she said to Angelica when she reached the fence. She slipped through the boards.

"The intruder did not come near us," Angelica replied. "We had a lovely night in a little clearing beneath a cliff." Her golden hair flashed in the early morning sun.

Ali laughed in amazement. "Your hair. It's blonde again," she said, incredulous.

Angelica made a face. "Yes," she said and grabbed a chunk of her hair in her hand. She looked at it disdainfully. "I wish it would stay that pretty chestnut color. It is so *bright* this way."

"I like it," said Ali. "It's sparkly, like it has glitter in it."

Angelica looked at Ali's hair. "I like yours better," she said. "It is almost the same color as Daydream, just a little darker. Now, how is Scruffy?"

"He's going to be fine," said Ali. "We're going to go pick him up at eight this morning."

"I am glad," answered Angelica. "Would you like to go for a ride while you wait?"

"I'd love to. Wait and I'll grab Daydream's bridle."

"There is no need. Here. I will give you a leg up," said Angelica.

"Okay," said Ali, her voice doubtful. "But I've never ridden without a saddle or bridle before."

"It is easy. I will show you."

Ali smiled. "It sounds like fun," she said and put her foot into Angelica's cupped hands. Ali settled onto the swayed back, grateful she still wasn't too heavy for the ancient mare. Her mom hadn't ridden Daydream for years, simply because she felt she was too big for Daydream to carry, but the old mare never seemed to have any trouble carrying Ali. Still, Ali was always careful to never ask Daydream to go faster than a walk.

"His shoulder isn't too stiff this morning. I'm glad, especially after that run they had last night," said Ali. She watched Angelica leap to Rhythm's back. Her hair instantly transformed into a warm golden brown. "Rhythm ran into a fence post when he was a year old, just playing and jumping around like young horses do sometimes," Ali explained. "And then the muscle atrophied – just wasted away. We tried everything to help him but we couldn't stop it. Doctor Blake says his shoulder will get worse the more he uses it."

"We will go slowly then," said Angelica. Rhythm turned effortlessly toward the back of the pasture and Daydream stepped in behind him. Crystal trotted around them in a circle, her tail in the air. She wove her head back and forth, tossing her mane, then kicked up her heels. Finally, her excess energy expended, she settled in behind Daydream.

"What did you find out last night?" asked Ali. "About the dog's owner, I mean." Her eyes turned to the trees from where the whistle had come.

"I followed the dog to where his mistress parked her car, but they had already left. I could tell nothing more than what Daydream has already told us. Afterward, I went to the horses. I was able to stay with them all night."

"It's too bad you didn't go back to the house for a few minutes," said Ali and Angelica turned on Rhythm's back to look at her. "A woman was there last night. Peter, my mom's boyfriend, saw her. I don't know if she was the intruder or not, but it makes sense that she was. She left right after he got there."

"Did he recognize her?" asked Angelica, her eyes alight.

Ali felt her forehead wrinkle in frustration. "He says he did. He said it was Maddie, my mom's friend. But it can't be. She and Mom have been best friends for years and I'm positive Maddie wouldn't do anything to hurt us. And the woman he saw wasn't driving Maddie's car either, so he has to be wrong."

"Are you sure?" asked Angelica. "Maybe she rents a car when she sneaks over here, so if anyone sees it, as Peter did, they will not recognize her."

Ali was silent for a moment as she stroked Daydream's neck. "Maddie can be irritating – I mean, she's *so* nosey – but I just can't see her doing something so horrible. She likes us. And she likes Scruffy and the horses."

But does she really? Ali suddenly wondered. *She almost never pets the horses when they're near her. It's like she thinks they'll give her fleas or something. And I don't think I've ever seen her touch Scruffy.*

"What is it?" asked Angelica. "You look worried."

"I really hope it's not Maddie," Ali said, shaking her head. "That would hurt Mom so much. She trusts her. She's always telling me Maddie's been there for her

62

through thick and thin, especially after my dad died. If the intruder was Maddie… " Ali left the sentence open. Words like disastrous and horrible seemed overly dramatic and yet, at the same time, not strong enough. Other than Ali, her mother trusted Maddie more than anyone else in the world.

Rhythm turned onto the trail to the wildflower meadow, Ali's favourite place to ride on the ranch. There was the occasional ring of hoof on stone as the horses climbed up a small, steep hill. Angelica and Ali leaned forward on their mounts. Rhythm made it up the hill in just a few jumps and Crystal climbed up easily behind him, but Daydream stopped halfway. Ali slid from her back. The old mare was breathing heavily. "Angelica!" she called. "We should go back. Daydream's tired."

"I will be right behind you," said Angelica from the top of the hill.

Ali grabbed Daydream's forelock. "Come on, girl. Let's go down." The mare lurched, stiff legged, down the short incline. At the bottom, she stopped to catch her breath. Ali looked up at Angelica on the gelding's back. "She's getting worse," she said, trying to keep the fear out of her voice. "She's always made it to the top before." Ali's fingers played with the old mare's forelock. The long hair was dry and for the millionth time, Ali noticed how gray her beloved horse was around her muzzle. Daydream nickered low in her throat and nuzzled Ali's shoulder.

Rhythm and Crystal clattered down the hill and stopped beside Daydream and Ali. Angelica jumped from Rhythm's back. "I don't think I'll ride her anymore," said Ali, turning to Angelica. "If I just take her for walks, she should get enough exercise to stay healthy, right? I couldn't bear it if anything happened to her." She looked into the mare's dark eyes and tried to swallow her sadness. "Our last ride, Daydream. That was our last ride."

"All creatures pass beyond this world, Ali," said Angelica, gently. She put her hand on Ali's shoulder.

Ali shrugged her hand away. "No! Not Daydream. She's going to live to be the oldest horse ever. I'm going to make sure of that." Even Ali was surprised at the intensity in her voice. Angelica looked down at the ground. "I... I'm sorry, Angelica," Ali stammered. "I didn't mean... I just... I would miss her way too much. She can't... die."

Angelica's golden eyes met Ali's. "I must tell you something, Ali. Something that will be hard for you to hear. When I came to the stable last night Daydream told me of the strange things that were happening around your home. She told me of the stranger and the tampered grain. But she also told me of another worry that has been consuming her."

Ali turned back to Daydream and touched the mare's lowered forehead with her own. Tears broke free from her eyes.

"She told me that she knows her time here is almost finished," continued Angelica. "And she is ready to go. But she worries that you are not ready to let her. She asked me to speak to you. To tell you that death is a natural part of life. That she will always live on in your memories and in your heart. That she is so proud of you and your mom, of her foals and grand-foals. That she has lived a rich and beautiful life. But now, it is time for her... "

"Stop!" Ali couldn't bear to hear any more. She rubbed the tears from her face with her sleeve. "Stop," she said again, her voice a hoarse whisper.

"I am sorry," said Angelica. She put her hand on Ali's shoulder again and this time Ali hardly noticed. Her body was shaking in her effort to hold back her sobs. She slumped against Daydream, suddenly dizzy. Daydream nuzzled her arm and a new spasm of grief washed over Ali. With a gigantic effort, she pushed her emotions back. Daydream *couldn't* die! She was old, true, but she was healthy. She would live for many years still. Ali had heard of horses that were more than forty and Daydream was barely over thirty years old.

She forced her face into an expressionless mask, then turned to Angelica. "Daydream won't die," she said forcefully. "She would never leave me when I need her so much. She's my best friend."

A sad smile appeared on Angelica's face. "And you are her best friend," she said. Rainbow tears glinted in her golden eyes. She reached out to stroke Daydream's side. "I have told you what Daydream wanted you to hear. There is no need to speak of it further."

By the time Angelica and Ali made it back to the main pasture, it was almost 7:30. Most of the walk back was silent with Ali walking at Daydream's side and Angelica following with the other two horses. When they came in sight of the house, Ali stopped and turned back. "Me and Mom will go get Scruffy pretty soon," she said. "Can you stay with the horses while we're gone and keep them safe?"

"Yes," said Angelica. "I will go with them to one of the back pastures again. Do not worry if you do not see us when you return."

"Thanks Angelica," said Ali. "And I'm sorry for acting mad at you. I wasn't really mad. Not really. I was just scared. I... " Angelica held up her hand and Ali stopped speaking.

"I know, Ali. I understand. There is no need to apologize."

"Thanks Angelica. I'll see you when we get back." Ali patted Daydream on the neck, then ran toward the house. She was eager to be in the car and on their way to pick up Scruffy. When she reached the fence she turned. Angelica was standing beside Daydream near the trees. She waved to Ali and Ali waved back, then the older girl led the horses into the trees. The old mare was the last to disappear beneath the forest canopy.

Ali felt a lump grow in her throat as Daydream faded into shadow. What if she did die? It would be so terrible. Another of the three central figures in Ali's life would be gone forever. First the father she could hardly remember, and then Daydream. Only her mom would be left. And what if something happened to her too, something like her starting to love Peter more than Ali?

No! I'm not going to think about that right now. I'll just think about Scruffy and about how Daydream's not going anywhere. About how we'll catch the intruder and how she won't be Maddie. And then how everything will be just like it always has been.

Ali raced toward the house. Within a matter of minutes, she had her mom in the car and they were on their way. First, they made a brief stop at the police station to report the vicious dog, then they continued on to the clinic.

The second they climbed out of the car, they could hear Scruffy howling. The secretary looked at them with relief when they said who they'd come to pick up. She gave Ali's mom the bill, chatting all the while as Shelley wrote a check from their horse fund. Ali tried to peek over her mother's shoulder as she wrote the check, but her mom blocked her view. Ali knew it was because her mom didn't want her to worry, but still she felt irritated. She had a right to know how much it cost, especially when the horses' futures could be at stake.

Scruffy was finally brought out. The vet's assistant carried him to their car and laid the dog on the back seat. Ali looked down at him with pity. His body was crisscrossed with slashes, cuts and bite marks, all evenly stitched together, and his broken leg was in a cast. Everywhere the veterinarian had stitched together a gash, Scruffy's hair was shaved and tufts of hair stood out between the stitches like strange gray sprouts.

"Stay there, Scruffy," said Ali and shut the car door. She hurried around to the front passenger side door and slid onto the seat. Scruffy was struggling to sit up. "Scruffy, lie down," she commanded, her voice firm. "I'm right here." Relieved, the dog collapsed on the seat, his eyes locked on Ali. He whined. "Don't worry, bud. We're taking you home right now. You'll feel better once you're at home." She reached over the seat and rubbed one of the long tufts on his side. "Poor, brave Scruffy," she whispered.

Daydream. You are tired. You should rest. This time has been such a strain for you. I will take you to your stall and give you some grain. You can sleep there in peace, knowing I am watching over you.

Crystal. Rhythm. I will stay with your dam. She needs me now. I suspect none will approach you during the daylight hours. The intruder has only come in the evening and the dark of night. I believe you can graze and replenish yourselves in peace. But keep to the hidden places. When Ali returns home, I will come and find you.

Please try to eat, Daydream, my love. Please, if not for yourself, then for Ali. She needs you still.

Ali's mom drove slowly back to the ranch. Ali rubbed Scruffy's side as they traveled and, as long as her hand was touching him, he lay with his eyes closed and his breath soft and unhurried.

"Oh good," said Shelley, when they drove in the driveway. "Maddie's here. She said she might come over. She can help us carry Scruffy inside."

Ali jerked her hand away and peered out the window. Maddie's little blue car was parked in front of the house. Ali could see her sitting on the steps. She suppressed a groan when she saw Maddie stand and wave to them. She'd want to know about everything that happened to Scruffy and she'd probably act all mad at Ali's mom for not calling her when they needed help. *But I can ask her about last night,* Ali realized.

The car stopped and Ali climbed out. "Should we fix up a bed for him beside the stove?" she asked her mom. Scruffy whined from inside the car. "Just a minute, Scruff," she said to the impatient dog.

"I'll do it, Ali," replied her mother. "He won't want to let you out of his sight until he's somewhere he feels safe. I think I'll get your old playpen from the basement to put him in. It's nice and soft and it'll stop him from moving around too much."

"Good idea." Ali opened the back door of the car and sat beside her dog. "See, Scruffy? We're home," she said. "In just a minute, we'll carry you inside."

Scruffy rolled onto his belly and looked at her with a sad expression. Ali noticed his eyes were clearer. He seemed more aware than he had at the clinic. "The anaesthetic is wearing off, isn't it, buddy? That's good." She stroked his head. "Mom got some pills for you. They'll help with the pain." Scruffy shuffled toward her across the seat and laid his head on her lap.

"Hi, Ali." Maddie's voice came from beside her and Ali jumped. Maddie giggled.

"I thought you went inside with Mom," said Ali, her voice slightly accusing.

"Sorry," said Maddie. "How's Scruffy?"

"He'll be okay," answered Ali. She glanced at the door to the house. Her mom was still inside. This was her chance. She fastened her eyes on Maddie's face. "Hey Maddie, why'd you come over last night?" she asked, trying to look as innocent as possible.

Surprise slid over Maddie's face. "What? What do you mean? I didn't come over last night." She laughed. "Why would I come over?"

"Peter said he saw you," Ali said with relief. She was so glad Maddie wasn't the intruder. Peter *was* wrong.

Then, suddenly, the color evaporated from Maddie's face. Her mouth opened in shock.

"What's wrong?" asked Ali. "Are you okay?" Maddie looked like she was ready to faint. Her bright red lips were garish in her pale face.

Maddie squeezed her eyes shut for a moment. Her knuckles turned white as she gripped the car door. She straightened. "I'm fine," she said in a nonchalant voice.

71

"Just a dizzy spell. I think I'm getting sick. I bet I have that flu that's going around." She coughed to emphasize that she wasn't feeling well.

Ali grimaced. The cough sounded so artificial. "So you *didn't* come over last night?" she persisted, trying to sound as casual as Maddie.

Maddie's eyes narrowed for a moment before she turned her head away and gazed toward the door to the house. She looked as if she was wishing Shelley would reappear. "Actually, now that you mention it, I did drop by for a second. I just forgot. When I heard about Scruffy, I was upset."

"So who's car were you driving?" asked Ali, innocently.

Maddie's mouth dropped open again. "Uh, a friend's," she answered. Then, "Oh Shelley, good!" Her voice was loud and aggressively cheerful. "I'll help you move Scruffy, the poor guy. Then we absolutely have to go down to the beach for a while. You need to relax a little. And Ali has to come with us. The girl is positively worn out."

Ali was thoughtful as she moved out of the way. She couldn't make sense of it. At first Maddie said no, she hadn't come over, and she seemed believable. Then she suddenly changed her mind but she acted so strange that Ali didn't know whether to believe her or not. Had Maddie come over the night before as she claimed? Was she the crazy intruder? So much depended on the answer. So much.

The woman climbed up the hill, the coiled rope and bridle gripped tightly in her sweaty hands. The horses had to be here somewhere. She'd checked all the bigger pastures and there was only one place left they could be. The wildflower meadow. Breathing heavily, she scrambled to the top of the incline. There in the dirt, fresh hoof prints.

She almost jumped for joy. Could she get any luckier? It was the perfect place: they couldn't escape from her here. There was an old gate that could close off the meadow and a catch pen at the other end. She could herd the horses inside, rope the gelding, and they would be on their way.

The woman broke over the top of the hill and jogged along the trail through the trees. At the entrance to the meadow, she stopped. The two horses saw her in the same moment she saw them. Instantly, the woman dropped the rope and bridle, and clasped her hands together over her heart. They were so lovely, just like glistening statues. She hated to disturb them, hated to destroy their perfect poses. Then the gelding stepped forward and whinnied.

"You like me," the woman said, enthralled. "Me. You like me. Me." The gelding stood still for another long moment, sniffing the wind, then turned uncertainly. Both horses trotted away, their heads and tails in the air. Halfway across the meadow, they stopped and looked back.

"My pretty ones, so pretty. So pretty," the woman sighed. The horses were glorious, the meadow was beautiful, and the warm breeze ruffling the wildflowers was intoxicating. The ranch was welcoming her home. It loved her. She felt like crying. She had dreamed of coming home for so long and now, finally, she felt welcome. Safe.

Suddenly, she jumped to the side. The gate to the meadow was still there but like everything else on Anela Ranch, it was falling apart. She jerked on the top rail and the entire gate broke away from rusty hinges and fell to the ground. The woman cursed and kicked the rotten wood, then looked back at the rope on the ground. It would be long enough. Quickly she strung the rope from one dilapidated gatepost to the other, and back. Only two thin lines between captivity and freedom, but it would be enough.

When she turned back to the horses, she couldn't believe her luck. They were watching her from just outside the catch pen. She walked toward them, her hand out. Slowly, the two edged back into the pen. When the woman reached the gate, she pushed it shut and laughed merrily.

"My pretties, my pretties," she said in a light voice. Then she turned and ran back to retrieve her rope. She skipped back to the catch pen, the rope coiled over her shoulder and the bridle in her hand. Now she just

needed to catch the gelding. It wouldn't be hard. He was a little nervous, but obviously didn't think she was too much of a threat. And why should he? She was doing him a favour.

"A favour," she crooned to the gelding in a singsong voice, as she shook out the lasso. "I'm doing you a favour. A favour."

Ali trailed behind Maddie and her mom as they carried Scruffy to the house. The two women talked about what they could take to the beach for a picnic lunch and didn't hear the "psst" that came from behind the group.

Ali turned to see Angelica waving at her from the corner of the closest shed. The blonde girl signalled to Ali to come to her.

"What is it? Is anything wrong?" The questions bubbled from Ali's mouth when she slipped into the shadow of the shed beside Angelica.

"No, nothing is wrong. Daydream is in her stall, resting. She is tired," said Angelica. Worry flashed across Ali's face and Angelica continued. "There is nothing wrong. I promise. I brought her here half an hour ago and she already feels better. She did not want to go to the wildflower meadow with Crystal and Rhythm."

Ali didn't feel much better. Daydream had never stayed behind the other horses before. It was just more evidence that she wasn't a young horse anymore, something Ali would rather forget.

"Now that you are home, I will go to Crystal and Rhythm," Angelica continued. "Can you stay with Daydream?"

"Yes. And Angelica, Maddie's here," Ali said, changing the subject. "Remember what Peter said about her coming over last night? Well, I asked her if she did. At first she was surprised and said no. And then she acted all weird and said yes."

A line appeared between Angelica's eyes. "What do you mean by weird?"

"She was surprised, *really* surprised. And..." Ali thought for a moment. Maddie had been surprised, true. But after the shock, there had been another emotion. A subtle, carefully hidden emotion that she'd stuffed beneath excessive cheerfulness. "Fear?" Ali said doubtfully. "Could she be afraid? But that makes no sense."

"Of what could she be afraid?" asked Angelica, puzzled.

"Maybe because Peter saw her here?" Ali said, even though she knew that couldn't be it. No, if it was fear, something else had frightened Maddie. But what? "She wants me to go to the beach with her and Mom and that's strange too," Ali said slowly. "I wasn't going to go, but maybe I should. Maybe I'll find out what's happening."

"That is a good idea," replied Angelica. "You can watch Daydream at the same time. She would like a stroll to the beach, as long as the path is not too strenuous."

"It isn't. There aren't any steep hills or anything."

"Then I am sure she would like a gentle amble, especially with you. Her time with you is very precious."

Ali blinked back abrupt tears. Why did Angelica keep saying things that made it sound like Daydream was going to die any second? "You're going to go find Crystal and Rhythm?" she asked to change the topic.

"Yes. I will guard Crystal and Rhythm, just in case our intruder is not Maddie. We must continue to be cautious until we know for sure."

Ali drew a deep breath. "I really hope it isn't her." She glanced back at the house. "I better go. Scruffy's probably wondering where I am."

"Then let us meet again tonight, in the stable," suggested Angelica. "We must think of what to do. We must find this intruder as soon as we can, for the sake of the horses."

Ali nodded. She knew better than anyone that they had to find the truth soon. Very soon. Every time the intruder tried to hurt the horses, there was a chance she would succeed, and the intruder's next attempt on the horses' lives could be the time she accomplished her goal.

The woman slid from the gelding's back. She approached the back fence with his reins clutched in her hand.

She pushed against the top board with all her strength. The nails pulled free of the fencepost with a loud squeal and the board bounced onto the ground. She pushed against the second board with her foot. It too, came away from the post. She didn't bother with the bottom board. The horse could step over it. Nimbly, she leapt back onto the gelding's bare back.

"Let's go, gimpy, gimpy," she said in a happy voice and dug her heels into his ribs. He leapt forward, startled, and already limping.

A plan began to come to Ali when she walked into the house to hear Maddie's high-pitched voice echoing from the kitchen. By the time she'd given Scruffy some water, she knew how to tell if Maddie was involved. She would casually mention to her mom, within Maddie's hearing, that she was keeping the horses in the stable that night just in case the dog came back. But instead, she'd put them in the garden shed where her mom kept the lawnmower, hoes, and rakes.

It was a perfect plan. The stable was the strongest building on the property and it only had one door. Both windows had shutters that could be barred on the outside. Ali and Angelica could bar the shutters over the windows, leave the stable door unlocked and wait to see if Maddie went inside to get to the horses. If she did, they could shut the door behind her and, once trapped, Maddie would be forced to explain.

Ali smiled. The plan was perfect, because, if Maddie were innocent, she wouldn't come to the stable at all.

She bent over the edge of the playpen and kissed Scruffy on the head. "I'll ask Angelica what she thinks about the plan first," she whispered to the injured dog. "Just think, Scruff. Tonight could be the night we catch the intruder." Scruffy laid his head on his unbroken leg and sighed contentedly. Ali smiled. The dog was happy to be home.

"I hope the mean dog doesn't come tonight," Ali whispered. Scruffy's eyes slowly closed as her fingers caressed his ears. "Or, if he does, that he goes into the stable with Maddie too." Gentle snores swelled around her and Ali straightened. Scruffy wouldn't mind if she went with her mom and Maddie for a while. He wouldn't even know. She listened to the murmur of the women's voices coming from the kitchen. They were packing a picnic lunch for their excursion to the beach.

From habit, Ali looked up before walking into the stable. Daydream whinnied to her, delighted. "How are you, magical moonflower horse?" said Ali, rubbing Daydream's white star. "Would you like to go to the beach for a while?" She took Daydream's halter from the hook outside her stall and slipped it over the mare's head, then led her old friend from the stall. At the door to the stable she stopped and reached into the grooming kit she kept there. She selected Daydream's favourite brush and stroked the dark brown neck. The mare groaned with pleasure and stretched her neck. Ali laughed and continued down the mare's side with brisk brush strokes. She quickly groomed Daydream's left side, then moved on to the right. Finally she combed out the long mane and tail. "All ready to go, girl?" she asked when she finished. "Mom and Maddie should be ready soon."

Ali left Daydream ground-tied by the backdoor to the house and went to find the two women. They were packing the last of the picnic lunch into a basket. Ali looked in on Scruffy before they left. He was still snoring. Ali stifled a giggle. As if he sensed her amusement, Scruffy fell silent. His legs twitched for a moment, then he lay still, his only movement being the steady rise and fall of his ribs. Ali tiptoed from the room.

"Daydream's coming too. Wonderful," said Ali's mom when they stepped outside.

"I thought she might have fun. You know how she loves playing in the waves. And Crystal and Rhythm took off to graze. I don't want her to be lonely."

"No explanations needed," said Ali's mom. "I love spending time with my beautiful wild moonflower horse." She leaned forward and kissed Daydream's forehead, right in the middle of her white star.

Maddie laughed beside her. "Aren't nicknames supposed to be shorter than the original name?" she asked.

Ali's mom coloured slightly. "I know it sounds silly, but, well, Daydream's special."

Inwardly, Ali groaned. *No Mom, don't tell her! She doesn't need to know everything about us.*

"What do you mean?" asked Maddie. The two women turned and walked toward the beach trail. Ali and Daydream fell in behind.

"When Daydream was born we didn't know if she and her dam would live. I was in the stable for almost two days, helping my mom and dad with them. It was awful. Anyway, Daydream's dam died, leaving her an orphan. It was so sad. We named her Daydream after her dam, so really she's Daydream the second, but she should have been called Moonflower."

"Why?" asked Maddie impatiently.

"It was the strangest thing. Dad picked her up and was carrying her to the house, and Mom and I were walking

82

behind. It was a hot, hot day and the sun was blasting down on us, and suddenly we all smelled this amazing smell. The wild moonflower vine climbing the outside of the stable was in full bloom, absolutely dripping with hundreds and hundreds of white flowers."

"But… " started Maddie.

"Yes, I know," laughed Ali's mom. Her peal of merriment swelled back to Ali and Daydream, and Ali smiled. "Moonflowers only bloom at night, under the moon," she continued. "See what I mean? Daydream's special. They bloomed for her, to welcome her into the world."

"What a cool story," said Maddie, glancing back at Daydream with new respect. "You should write it down and sell it. You could make some extra money that way."

The basket swung between the two women as they continued walking and Ali dropped back a bit further. It *was* a cool story. And maybe Maddie was on to something. Ali knew her mom was smart. If she wrote the story about Daydream and the moonflowers, she was sure someone would want to publish it. Maybe she would even make enough money to keep Crystal's next foal. That would be so wonderful.

"You really should go to Marshall to get your hair done." Maddie's voice drifted back to Ali. Apparently the topic of conversation had changed. "He's fantastic." Maddie tossed her dark curls.

"Maybe next month," said Ali's mom.

Maddie laughed. "No you won't. I know you. If you have any extra money at all, it'll go to the ranch. You really should sell this place, Shelley. It's too hard on you to keep it and think of all the things you could buy." A tense note was creeping into Maddie's voice. "You'd have tons and tons of money. Ali would love it."

Shelley shook her head. "I wouldn't be too sure about that," she said.

Ali picked up her pace. "Come on Daydream," she whispered. "Mom, are you planning on swimming?" she asked, hoping it was enough to redirect the conversation.

"Of course. Aren't you?"

"I forgot my swim suit," said Ali.

"Well, we're going to have lunch first anyway. And you can't swim for a while after you eat, so you can run back up to the house and get it then, okay?"

Maddie began to describe the new bikini she was wearing under her clothes to Shelley and irritation swarmed over Ali. She bit back a remark about Maddie wearing a bikini when she *apparently* had the flu. She stopped and pretended to adjust Daydream's halter, then ran her fingers through Daydream's heavy mane as she waited for the women to get farther ahead. "I hate it when she tries to talk Mom into selling the ranch," she confided in the old mare.

Soon they were at the beach. Maddie spread the blanket over the black unmarked sand and Shelley sat down and pulled the sandwiches out of the basket.

"Is there anything for Daydream?" asked Ali, wishing she'd remembered earlier. She knelt down beside her mom.

"Well, let's see." Shelley pulled out the juice and some cups, then some apples. She handed two to Ali. "She can have mine. I'm not very hungry."

"Thanks, Mom." Ali put the largest apple on the palm of her hand and held it out to Daydream. The mare took the apple in her teeth and bit it neatly in two, letting half of it fall into the sand. She stared out at the lapping waves as she chewed. Ali took a bite of her apple.

"I'm serious, Shelley," Maddie piped up again. "You *should* think of selling the place. You'd be so rich. Just imagine. Owning the only access to this beach is worth a fortune, let alone all the other stuff, the fields, the forests, the heritage house – and the best part is that then I'd be the friend of a rich lady and we could go on holidays to Italy together." Both women laughed and then Maddie continued, her voice unnaturally strained. "By the way, Shelley, just out of curiosity, have you received any more big offers lately?"

Ali couldn't take any more. She grabbed the other half of Daydream's apple and jumped to her feet. "I have to wash it off," she said in an unsuccessful attempt to sound polite. She strode toward the water, Daydream close behind her. Why was Maddie being so insistent? She'd mentioned selling their property twice today and she'd been there less than an hour. What was wrong with her?

Ali held the washed apple out to Daydream. When the mare took the treat in her worn teeth, Ali wiped her wet hand on her shorts. "Come on, Daydream," she said. "Let's take a walk down the beach. I've got to get away from her."

They splashed through the water. The tide was low and Ali kept stopping to look at different shells that had washed up during high tide. She found a perfect tiny cowry shell and held it in her hand as they walked, rubbing its satin smoothness with her fingers. The water was warm on her feet, the sand hot. Soon, the voices faded in the distance. Ali looked back. Her mom and Maddie were still sitting on the blanket, talking. They were too far away for Ali to see their expressions, but Maddie was gesturing with her hands. Shelley threw back her head and laughed and after a second, Maddie joined her. Ali turned away.

She was almost to the headlands, the rocks that would stop Daydream from going any further. Ali scrambled up the first of the rocks and sat down. Daydream stood beside her on the sand and the two of them stared at the black rocks stretching far out into the water, the residue of a volcanic explosion from eons before. At the tip of the headland, waves pounded against the ancient lava.

A tiny rock clattered beside Ali and she and Daydream looked at it curiously. Then another small black rock hit the sand near Daydream's hindquarters. Ali spun around. Angelica was standing at the edge of the forest crowding the beach, waving to her. Ali jumped from the rock and trotted toward the golden girl. When she heard Daydream breathing heavily behind her, she slowed to a walk.

"Ali!" Angelica's voice sounded panicky.

The cold ice of fear crackled up Ali's spine and she stopped. What was wrong? She glanced at her mom and Maddie, far down the beach. They were still totally engrossed in their conversation. They hadn't seen or heard Angelica.

"The horses are gone!"

Ali felt the perfect cowry shell slip from her fingers. It dropped to the sand without a sound.

The woman kicked the gelding again. His limp was getting worse with every lurch up the volcano's side. She felt so bad for him. He was in such pain. But his suffering will soon be over. "Let's go, gimpy," she murmured in her most encouraging tone.

The gelding stumbled and almost fell, catching himself just before falling to his knees. The woman slipped from his back and hurried to stroke his face.

"Poor gimpy boy. Come on, gimpy boy. You've got to try harder. I know it hurts. But if you just try harder, harder, the pain will be over sooner. Really. Sooner. I promise. Trust. Trust me." She kissed him on his nose and stroked his blaze. "Try harder. Harder."

A flash of color in the trees behind the horse. The mare! She was following. "Come on," she said to the gelding in her most convincing voice. "We have to go. And hurry. Hurry. You don't want your sister coming too close. Neither of us wants that. Do we? Do we?"

She pulled on the reins, leading him forward. The gelding stepped after her, his shoulder quivering under his own weight as he dug his hooves into the steep hillside.

Ali walked casually back toward her mom and Maddie, using all her self-control to not break into a run. She couldn't let her mother or Maddie suspect anything, and besides, it was too hard for Daydream to trot in the sand. She kept close to the water where the sand was harder and it was easier for Daydream to walk, then cut up toward the trail to the house. When she was near the trail, she heard her mom call. She turned back and waved.

"I'm going to get my swimsuit," she yelled. "But if I don't come back, don't worry. I might stay with Scruffy." She reached out to touch Daydream's neck. Good. The mare wasn't overheating.

"Okay, sweetie," her mom called back and Ali turned toward the trail again.

"Oh, Ali, come back, okay?" yelled Maddie. "I wanted to spend this day with you too."

Ali pretended she didn't hear and kept walking, but Maddie's words disturbed her. Her mom's friend had never cared if Ali spent time with her on other days. Before all the weird things started happening around the ranch, Ali would've just thought Maddie was in a strange mood. But now she wondered. She broke into a light jog once they were on solid ground. The stable yard fence drew nearer and nearer and finally she was there. Angelica ran toward them, her hair flying behind her like a golden cape.

"Hurry, Ali. Help me get Daydream into her stall." Angelica flung the stable door wide. Ali rushed into the stable and opened Daydream's stall door. But Daydream hadn't followed her. She was standing outside the stable beside Angelica, shaking her head back and forth. Angelica reached for the old mare's forelock and tugged gently. "Come on, old girl," she murmured. "You cannot help us this time." With a sigh, Daydream followed her into the stable.

With Daydream safe in her stall, the two girls sprang into action. Angelica led the way across the large pasture at a run, with Ali right behind her.

"What happened, Angelica?" Ali panted as she tried to keep up.

"The intruder has taken the horses."

For a second, Ali slowed. The severity of what that meant made her feel weak, almost sick. If the intruder had the horses and she and Angelica weren't fast enough to save them, they would be in serious trouble. She and Angelica were their only chance of survival. She had to run faster, somehow she had to run faster. "Didn't you say they can call you to help them? Why don't they?"

"I do not know," Angelica yelled back. She wasn't even breathing hard. "Maybe they do not know she is the intruder. They were not in the stable with Daydream when the grain was left there. They may not understand she is a threat to them."

Within minutes they were in the wildflower meadow. Angelica ran straight toward a hole in the fence and jumped nimbly over the bottom rail. Ali looked in despair at the thick brush beneath the trees. "How are we going to track them? We can't tell where they've gone," she said between gasps.

"I can feel the energy left in their passing." Angelica glanced back for a moment. "The energy of the intruder is very strange: kind and heartfelt. It is as if she now believes she is doing something good for the horses." She slipped soundlessly into the undergrowth. The leaves hardly quivered in her passing.

"Because she's crazy," Ali gasped and followed as quickly as she could. She knew she was at least ten times louder than Angelica as she ran through the bush. *But it doesn't matter,* she told herself. *I've just got to be fast. We've got to catch them as soon as we can. Before they get to their destination, where ever that is.*

They came to a steep incline and, to Ali's surprise, Angelica went straight up the volcanic slope, grabbing branches to help pull herself upward. Ali followed for a short distance, then called to Angelica to stop. "Are you sure they went this way?" she asked, breathlessly.

"There are marks on the ground," said Angelica, pointing to Ali's feet.

Ali looked. Dark earthy scratches marred the forest floor where the horses had scrambled up the steep section. "But it makes no sense," she gasped. "Why toward the volcano? She can't make them jump inside or anything."

Suddenly Ali felt faint. She knew where the intruder was taking the horses. The sulphur field. If the intruder felt so *kindly* toward the horses, she wouldn't want to murder them herself. No, she would let the poisonous gasses do it for her. And it wouldn't look like murder either. Everyone would think the horses broke out of the pasture and wandered into the sulphur field by chance. A strange and tragic accident, that's all. All the intruder would have to do is ride them into the center of that barren wasteland where nothing could survive, leave them to breath the poisoned air, and they would die.

"What is it, Ali?" Angelica slid down the hill. Her eyes flashed as Ali explained. "We must hurry," she said when Ali finished. "We must save them." She began to climb up the hill, a new desperation in her movements.

"Wait," called Ali. "Don't go that way. I know a shortcut. Come on! Follow me!"

The woman rode the gelding onto the barren yellowed ground. She smelled the sulphur and felt the burning in her lungs in the same second the gelding stopped short. He tried to turn away but she held tight to the reins. She reached into the pocket of her jacket and grabbed the gasmask she'd brought with her. She put it on, then slipped from the gelding's back and led him forward. He took another lurching step and stopped again.

Slowly her lips curled upward beneath her mask. "I know what will help you, gimpy boy," she said, in her most soothing voice. "We'll make this as easy as we can, okay? Okay? Just relax. You'll feel better, better, in a few minutes. No more pain. A favour. Favour."

She slipped her jacket off and eased it over his head, then tied the sleeves under his throatlatch, completely blindfolding him. Then she turned him in a circle. Just as she suspected, he followed. He had to depend on her now that he was blind. She turned him around and around in limping, lurching circles until she was sure he'd lost his sense of direction. Then she patted him one more time on his atrophied shoulder and led him into the poisoned gasses.

Ali led Angelica up the trail at a run. They had to get to the sulphur vents before it was too late. They had to save the horses. *If it isn't too late already,* thought Ali as she ran.

When she saw the opening in the hillside, she stopped and pointed. "Lava tube," she said between gasps. "Faster that way. Cuts through ridge." She put her hands on her knees and tried to catch her breath.

"Come when you can," said Angelica and ran up the hillside. Ali looked up in time to see her disappear into the round opening.

"Come on, Ali," she whispered to herself. "There's no time to rest. Get going." She grabbed a branch and with both hands, pulled herself up the hill toward the lava tube. Finally, she stumbled into the shady darkness of the tube.

A hundred years ago or more, molten lava, moving through the cooling lava around it, had created this tube. The outer lava had hardened, become stiff, but the hottest lava kept pouring along its channel – until it poured right out the other end, leaving a tunnel through the earth.

Ali could see the distant daylight at the other end of the long tube. Angelica's form bobbed in front of the light as she ran. She didn't seem to be hindered by the darkness at all. It was as if she had the eyes of a cat. Ali hurried after her, moving as quickly as she could, ducking down whenever she came to a low spot in the ceiling. The last thing she wanted to do was run into the jagged rock outcroppings scattered along the ceiling of the lava tube. They weren't called sharktooth stalactites for nothing.

The lava tube was gaining in elevation. Ali felt ready to collapse. Her side was killing her and her breath was coming in harsh gasps. But she couldn't stop. She couldn't waste a single second. She kept her eyes fastened on Angelica's distant figure, outlined against the light.

Then suddenly, Angelica wasn't there anymore. *She must be through,* thought Ali. She faltered for a moment, stumbled. *But how can she run that fast? I must be slower than I thought.*

Ali forced her legs to move faster, her feet to step higher, her eyes to find the stalactites in the gloom before she bumped her head on them. She didn't have time to trip and she certainly couldn't get injured. The daylight grew slowly in front of her. She was almost halfway through the tube. She had to run faster. Faster. Somehow faster.

The gelding's coughing was horrible to hear. The woman felt so terrible for him. She pulled her jacket from his head and threw it over her shoulders. Then she slipped the bridle off him. No matter how badly she felt, there was no point in losing a good bridle. She had just pulled the spade bit from the horse's mouth, when he sunk to the ground, his sides heaving as he gasped for clean air. His coughing was tearing his body apart.

"Good gimpy, good boy. Boy," she murmured and patted him on his neck. Then she hurried away. At the edge of the sulphur field, she tossed her mask. She looked back at the quivering mass that had once been a horse, and smiled. Just a few more minutes and he would feel no more pain. He would be free.

She started to jog away. It was quite a distance to where she'd left her car and she didn't want to leave Wolf for too long. He would miss her too much.

Angelica

Crystal. You summoned me. Thank you! Now tell me what is happening. Where is Rhythm?

Oh no.

Quickly, let me ride on your strong back. We must get to him before it is too late!

Ali

Ali burst from the lava tube and cupped her hands around her mouth. "Angelica!" No answer. Ali didn't wait to call again. She raced up the slope and through the trees. The trees were thinning ahead and the ground was flattening out. She was getting close to the sulphur field. Nothing would grow in that poisoned air; no living thing could survive there for long. And that's where the intruder had taken Rhythm, she was sure.

Somehow she found the strength to run faster, though her body was already starving for air. She leapt over logs and darted around brush patches in an effort to get there faster. Even seconds could count. And she would never forgive herself if she could have made it to Rhythm's side in time and didn't.

The trees finally fell away and Ali wove her way through the sickly looking brush at the edge of the sulphur field, her eyes sharp for any sign the horses had been there. Or Angelica, though the fact she couldn't see Angelica made her feel a little better.

Please, God, make Angelica be with Crystal and Rhythm right now, she prayed. *Please help her save them both in time. And Crystal's baby too. Please, please.*

Angelica

Crystal, stay back where you and your unborn foal will be safe. I will go to Rhythm alone. I can go safely into the poisonous gasses because of the mask the intruder left behind.

Please Crystal, do not mourn him. Not yet. I will do everything I can to bring him back to you. Everything. We must both pray it is enough.

At the edge of the sulphur field, Ali came to a quick stop. She couldn't believe her eyes. It was the worst scenario she could have imagined, come true. Rhythm had collapsed in the most gaseous, most dangerous part of the sulphur field. Even from a distance Ali could see the yellow smears on his coat, evidence of his struggles to climb to his hooves after he had fallen. But he was still now. Deathly still.

Tears sprung from Ali's eyes and suddenly she couldn't see. Rhythm couldn't be dead. Not her Rhythm, her beautiful, patient, loving Rhythm. She stepped forward blindly. She had to get to him. Maybe it wasn't too late. Maybe there was still a chance he could rise up and follow her back to the forest. She coughed violently when the first of the sulphur entered her lungs.

"Ali, no! Stop! Go back!" Angelica's voice was barely audible above Ali's hacking coughs. She dashed her tears away to see Angelica halfway across the sulphur field, the lower half of her face covered by a mask. "Go to Crystal and wait there. I will get him. Do not worry," Angelica yelled.

Ali looked to where Angelica pointed. Crystal was at the edge of the sulphur field to her right, tossing her head up and down and looking like she too, wanted to run to Rhythm's side. With a huge effort, Ali stuffed down her longing to be with Rhythm. Crystal needed her as well. And Angelica had a mask. She could go to Rhythm safely.

Ali ran toward the chestnut mare. "Crystal," she called. The mare looked at her for a moment and neighed. The sound was long and searing. Then she turned her eyes back to Rhythm. Ali reached Crystal's side and her hand went automatically to the mare's silken neck as she turned to watch Angelica.

The older girl had reached Rhythm's side. Ali watched her bend over the gelding's head. She looked like she was whispering in his ear. Suddenly she straightened. "He is still alive!" she yelled back to Ali and Crystal. Relief flooded through Ali and she threw her arms around Crystal's neck. She shoved her face into the mare's mane and drew a deep breath.

Thank you, God! Thank you, thank you, thank you! The tears threatened to start again. *Not yet, now isn't the time!* she commanded herself fiercely. *Rhythm or Angelica might still need me. I can't just dissolve into tears! Not yet.*

Ali rubbed her eyes and turned back to watch Angelica. The girl was kneeling between Rhythm's head and his forelegs. Her right hand was on his heart, her left on his head. Her head was bowed and bright hair fell over the gelding's neck, mingling with the golden chestnut.

Suddenly Angelica shuddered, a violent shudder that Ali could see, even from yards away. The girl turned her eyes up toward the sky and Ali saw the sparkle of tears pouring down her face.

100

He's dead. Ali knew it as well as if it were her own hand over the gallant horse's heart. Rhythm had given out. He could hold on no longer. The poisoned gas had destroyed his lungs.

Blinded by tears of grief, Ali turned to Crystal and hugged the mare to her. "It's okay, girl, it's okay," she murmured over and over, even though she knew it wasn't. Things could never be okay again. Rhythm was dead. Gone forever. Nothing now but the beloved memory of a bright and sparkling colt, galloping across the fields, his head high and his eyes alight with joy. After the accident that lamed him, Ali and her mom had discovered his infinite patience. His trust in them. His kindness and gentleness. He was truly a horse in a million.

And now he was gone. She would never feel his warmth again. Never hear him nicker to her when she entered the stable. Never again sit on his broad, strong back. The intruder had stolen him from them. He was gone. Forever.

Great One. It is not time for Rhythm to leave us. He is needed here still. Please send him back to Ali and her mother, to Crystal and Daydream. Please hear me. Please listen, I beg you.

I will give him what I can. All I am, if needed. I will give my life for his, Great One. Without question. Without hesitation. I would consider it an honour.

Please, Great One. Hear my plea and have mercy on this innocent one. Send life to him once again.

Ali

Ali felt him beside her. Rhythm. Like a silent whisper, speaking to her heart. She jerked away from Crystal, dashed the tears from her eyes and looked around. There was no ghost horse. The scene was the same as it had been moments before, Angelica bending over Rhythm's lifeless body. Yet some thing, some tiny thing, was different.

Desperately, Ali shut her eyes. Yes, he was still there. She could still feel him. "Rhythm?" she whispered and reached out. Her fingertips tingled. "Don't go." Beside her Crystal nickered low in her throat. A plea. Then just as suddenly, he was gone. Ali felt a tugging at her heart. She didn't know what else to call it. It was like something was pulling at her insides, at her energy.

"Rhythm?" Ali said, a little louder. She opened her eyes, though she knew she wouldn't be able to see him. And her mouth dropped open.

Light streamed from Crystal's chest, from the forest, from every living thing in sight. Streamed toward Angelica. Toward Rhythm's body. Ali looked down. A tiny stream of light came from her own heart as well.

Fear abruptly choked her and the light disappeared. The tugging stopped. She took a deep breath and watched the other light particles flow toward Angelica, then touch her. Surround her. Add to her own glowing.

Suddenly, Angelica's body erupted in light. She threw her head back as the light travelled down her arms. Pure light surged from her hands, making them appear almost transparent, and spread in ripples over Rhythm's body. And Ali suddenly understood. Angelica was healing Rhythm. Either he wasn't dead or she was bringing him back!

Ali opened her heart to the tugging. The result was instantaneous. She looked down to see light burst from her own chest. It reached Angelica in moments and flowed along her arms to Rhythm. The horse was glowing as much as Angelica now and, as the girl of light sunk lower over his side, he raised his head. Ali wanted to cry with joy. Rhythm was alive!

The gelding rolled onto his stomach and Angelica slumped over his back. Ali could see the glow fading as the older girl lost strength.

"Hurry, Rhythm," she called, the urgency of the situation making her voice strong. "Come to me and Crystal! Hurry!" The two had to get out of the sulphur field before the glowing stopped. Rhythm still wouldn't be able to breathe the poisonous gases. He needed Angelica's light to protect him. And it was fading. Fast.

Cautiously, the gelding rose to his hooves. With the last of her energy, Angelica gripped his mane and then he was walking toward Ali and Crystal with careful steps, the girl draped across his back.

He coughed.

The glowing was almost completely gone now.

They need more protection. More light. Ali looked down. Only a thin stream of light was coming from her heart now. With Angelica unconscious, there was no one to direct the light to Rhythm. A thin glowing emanated from Crystal and nothing came from the surrounding forest anymore. Rhythm hacked again. And again. The sound was brutal in the unnatural hiss of the sulphur field.

Ali closed her eyes. Maybe Angelica couldn't pull it toward herself and Rhythm anymore but Ali could push it – or she was going to try anyway. She didn't dare look to see if it was working, but pushed harder. She had to send them more power.

Ali felt herself become weak. She reached out blindly and gripped Crystal's long mane. The mare nickered beside her, a worried sound, and her muzzle brushed Ali's cheek. Ali didn't dare open her eyes. If her efforts weren't working, she couldn't bear to see Rhythm fall again. She shoved the image of him sinking down into the yellow dust from her mind. She had to believe it was working. He couldn't die. She wouldn't let him!

Then she heard his hooves on the stones. He was there. Her eyes sprang open and she rushed forward to hug him. She grabbed Angelica just as she slipped from Rhythm's back and gently lowered her to the ground. The girl's hair lay around her like a white cloud, all color drained away.

She bent over the fallen girl. "Angelica?" she whispered. Then louder, "Angelica. Can you hear me?"

Ali looked up at Rhythm standing over her. "She'll be okay, won't she, Rhythm?" she asked, stricken. "She didn't have to give her life to save yours. Did she?"

Ali pulled the mask away from Angelica's porcelain face and placed her hand above the older girl's mouth and nose. There was a warm tickle against her palm. Angelica was breathing. She was still alive.

Ali shook the girl's shoulder. "Angelica, wake up. Rhythm's alive. You saved him. But you have to live too." There was a soft nicker behind her. "What do I do?" asked Ali, looking up at Rhythm. She wished the horses could answer her. There was the thud of hooves as Crystal moved to the other side of Angelica. The mare lowered her head and sniffed at the pale hair.

Rhythm pushed Ali gently with his muzzle. "What?" asked Ali and looked up at him. The gelding nuzzled Ali for a moment, then moved to touch Angelica's face. Ali blinked back tears as she watched the two horses.

"We've got to do something," she whispered. "She might die if we don't help her. But I don't even know what's wrong with her." She reached out and took Angelica's hand in hers. It was so cold, like ice. Ali rubbed it between her palms. "Angelica, wake up," she whispered again. "You have to wake up."

It was then she noticed the tears running down Rhythm's face. Her mouth dropped open. *Horses don't cry,* she thought. *Do they?* But Crystal was crying too. There was no mistaking it. Tears were spilling from both the horses' eyes, making dark, cascading rivulets down their faces. The tears dropped onto Angelica's cheek. Ripples of color washed over her alabaster skin.

Angelica drew in a deep breath. More tears fell and Ali felt warmth creep into the slim hand. Then Angelica opened her golden eyes. "Ali?" she whispered.

"I'm here," said Ali, leaning forward.

"What happened? Is Rhythm okay?"

"He's fine. You got him out in time."

A puzzled expression crossed Angelica's face and she pushed herself up on her elbows. "I did? I did not think we would make it," she said. Her voice was regaining strength.

"What happened?" asked Ali.

"Rhythm was dying and I tried to save him by giving him my light," explained Angelica, weakly. "But it was not enough, so I asked the Great One for help. And the Great One in turn, called upon the living things around us to give, if they so chose. Many gave some of their light, their life force."

"Freaky."

Angelica smiled. "Yes. *Freaky.* I like that word." A small tinkle of laughter. Ali relaxed even more. If Angelica was laughing, she had to be all right. The older girl climbed to her feet, then held her hand out to Ali. "I gave all I could for as long as I could, and I directed the life force of those who gave. But still, it did not seem to be enough. Then I do not know what happened. Everything went dark. Yet somehow we made it out of the sulphur fields." She looked at Ali with a level gaze. "Do you know what happened, Ali?"

"I, uh… " Ali looked down at the ground.

"Ali?"

"I pushed some light to you," she finally admitted. "That's all. Anyone would have done it."

Angelica shook her head. "No, Ali," she said slowly. "Not anyone. I am grateful. And so are Rhythm and Crystal. I will never forget."

Ali looked up and a small smile slipped across her face. "I don't make a very good hero," she said. "I never know what to say when people thank me."

"Me either," admitted Angelica. She wrinkled her nose. "So I do *not* thank you. And you cannot thank me, either."

"But that's not fair," protested Ali. "You saved Rhythm's life. You gave him your light and…" She stopped when Angelica raised an eyebrow. "Okay, okay, I see your point," she said and laughed.

"And I thank you, my loves," Angelica said and touched Crystal's cheek, then stroked Rhythm's blaze. "I owe you my life."

"How?" asked Ali, her voice puzzled.

"They cried over me because they love me, and their love, given in the form of tears, cured me."

"None of this makes any sense," said Ali, shaking her head. "Horses don't cry and it's impossible for them to cure you."

"It is as impossible for them to cure me as it is for us to cure Rhythm. Yet here he stands right now, living, breathing proof, so I would say it *is* possible."

All Ali could do was shake her head. She couldn't argue with such logic. Rhythm had been saved. And so had Angelica.

"And Rhythm has been given another gift," added Angelica. "Have you noticed yet?"

Ali's eyes skipped from Angelica to Rhythm. He looked exactly the same. Her gaze stopped at his shoulder. No, he wasn't exactly the same. The shoulder was plumper than it used to be. It looked like it did before the muscle had wasted away. Could it be?

"He's cured?" she whispered, almost afraid to say it out loud. Her hands touched the firm muscle. "His shoulder's been fixed?" She gasped and turned to Angelica. "It has, hasn't it?" Without waiting for an answer, she leapt toward Angelica, pulling the older girl into a crushing hug. "You did it!"

"We did it," corrected Angelica.

Ali spun toward Rhythm. "I can't believe it. It's so amazing!" she said as she reached for the gelding's face. "Your whole life will change now, Rhythm. Now you can run without anything hurting, like you did when you were young. You can jump and buck and twist and gallop all you want, and it will never, ever hurt again." She felt tears prickle her eyes again, tears of joy.

"Ali, we should start back. It will take some time to ride home, even if Rhythm is cured. And you used a lot of energy to help us. We must go slowly until your energy is replenished. Unfortunately, the horse's tears will not restore you. Only time will help."

"I do feel a bit weak still, but I don't care," Ali said, her voice still bubbling over with joy. "It's so awesome about Rhythm. I can't wait to see what he's like to ride now that he's not lame."

"Then you must ride him home," said Angelica.

"And on the way home, I'll tell you my plan," said Ali, her face losing some of its animation. They had thwarted the intruder's most recent attempts, but she knew it wasn't over yet. "I think I know how we can find out if Maddie's involved or not."

They walked the horses most of the way home. Even with everything that was happening, Ali couldn't help but feel exhilarated. Rhythm was cured! He didn't favour his leg at all and his stride was long and free. Powerful. He pranced in place behind Crystal when Angelica asked her to stop at the hole in the fence.

"Look at him, Angelica," said Ali. "He feels so wonderful! It must be totally incredible for him now, after being in pain for so many years."

Angelica slipped from Crystal's back. "It is wonderful," she agreed, with a broad smile. She patted Crystal on the rump and the mare jumped over the broken fence back into the pasture. Ali rode Rhythm forward and he jumped after his sister. "He will be a good horse for you, Ali."

Ali grinned. A horse to ride again, and ride fast, if she wanted. Crystal was always either in foal or had a foal at side, or both, and she couldn't ride Daydream fast.

Or at all, anymore, Ali remembered. *But she deserves a rest. I'll just take super good care of her and, when I want to ride, I can ride Rhythm. And I'm going to want to ride a lot!*

She slid from Rhythm's bare back. "We need a rock or something to pound the nails back in," she said and looked down at the boards the intruder had pushed from the post. Her eyes searched the ground and fell on a rounded stone. "Here." She picked up the rock and Angelica hoisted up the end of the board lying on the ground. Ali hit the nail head a few good strokes with the rock and the board was attached to the post again. She wiggled it. It was still loose.

"Do you have more nails at home?" asked Angelica.

Ali nodded. "I can bring some," she said. "I'll bring a bunch, just in case there are more loose boards."

"I will stay here with the horses," said Angelica. "If Maddie is involved, it will be better if she does not see them. They are safe only if she thinks they are dead."

"I'll be back as soon as I can. I want to check on Scruffy too. And Maddie might still be there. It's a good time to set our trap." Ali hugged Rhythm and Crystal one more time before she ran into the wildflower meadow. Partway across, she stopped and looked back. Angelica was sitting in the soft forest herbs and Crystal was lowering herself to lie beside her. But not Rhythm. He danced around them, tossing his head and arching his neck. Ali could hear Angelica's soft laugh float toward her. Her hand went out to stroke Crystal's red neck. It was such an enchanted scene. So peaceful. So safe looking.

But we're not safe, Ali reminded herself sternly. *Not yet. Not until we catch the intruder.* She turned to run toward home.

Scruffy's tail hit the mattress of the playpen, thump, thump, thump, when Ali walked into the room. "Hey, buddy," she murmured and leaned inside to rub the dog's undamaged ear. "How're you doing?" All of his water was gone. "Good boy!" Ali glanced at the clock above the mantle. "You want to try some food, Scruff? The vet said you could eat this afternoon."

"Ali?" Her mom's voice came from the kitchen.

"Yeah, Mom."

"What happened to you?"

"Oh nothing," said Ali, walking to the kitchen door. Maddie sat across the table from Ali's mom, a cup of coffee in her hand. "I just went to look for Crystal and Rhythm, but…." Ali let her voice trail away pathetically and tried to look as troubled as possible.

"What? What is it?"

"Oh nothing," said Ali, feeling bad she had to do this to her mother. She went to the cupboard that held Scruffy's food and put a handful in his dish, then ran some warm water from the tap to moisten it.

"Did you find them?" asked Maddie, sounding short of breath.

Ali turned away from the sink. Maddie's face was pale. "No," she said, her voice weak and sad. "But they might be up in one of the back meadows. I didn't check all of them."

"I'm sure they're fine, Ali," said her mom.

Then Ali put out the hook. The one they needed Maddie to hear. The one that would entice her to come around that evening, if she really was the killer. "I'm going to leave Daydream in the stable tonight, just in case, Mom," she said. "I don't want her wandering about if that dog comes back."

"That's a good idea, honey," said Ali's mom.

Two worry lines materialized between Maddie's eyes, just for a moment. Then, as if she suddenly realized Ali was watching her, she smoothed her forehead. "Well, I better get going, Shelley," she said, her voice falsely bright. "I can't waste the whole day having fun." She gulped down the last of her coffee and stood.

Ali filled Scruffy's water dish as Maddie was saying goodbye, then carried the two dishes into the living room and placed them carefully inside Scruffy's playpen, within his reach. He took a morsel of food and chewed it slowly, then lapped up a bit more water. The front door closed and a few seconds later, Ali heard Maddie honk her car horn as she drove out of the driveway. When Scruffy was finished, Ali pulled the food and water away from his nose so he wouldn't accidentally spill them and hurried back into the kitchen.

"Mom, would it be okay if I slept in the stable tonight with Daydream?" she asked hopefully. She needed to be allowed to stay outside, if their plan was going to work.

Ali's mom picked up her coffee from the table and sipped at it. "Sure, honey," she said after lowering her cup. "But you have to come in for an hour at least. Peter's coming for dinner tonight, since he missed last night."

Ali stopped her impulse to roll her eyes just in time. Actually it would be good if Peter came over. He and her mom would probably spend the evening talking or watching a movie on TV. Peter would keep her mother from checking up on Ali throughout the evening.

She would be left free to catch the intruder.

Evening was coming on. The woman whistled to Wolf as she walked out of her private rental cabin and instantly, he was there, a hulking black shadow at her heels. "Good boy, Wolfie Wolf Wolf," she murmured and thought of petting him on the head.

She opened the back door of the car for him and he leapt inside. The last of the dying light caught on his teeth and, for the first time, she wondered about climbing in the front seat with those slavering jaws behind her. She shrugged away the image. She was being silly. Wolf would never hurt her.

She started the car and backed carefully down the driveway. It was time to strike the next and final blow. The old mare.

Daydream entered the garden shed behind Ali. Angelica was already in the corner of the shed, spreading out a fresh bed of straw. She fluffed the last flake and stepped aside for Daydream.

"Where's the lawnmower?" asked Ali, looking around the shed in amazement. "And all the rakes and stuff?"

"I moved most of it outside," said Angelica. "I hope your mother does not mind."

"She won't even know. I'll move it back after tonight," said Ali.

Angelica hung the hay net in the corner of the Daydream's stall. "Do you have a bucket for fresh water?" she asked Ali.

"Sure. I'll get it for her." Ali was back in a couple of minutes with a bucket brimming with cool, clear water. She paused in the doorway of the garden shed. Angelica was grooming Daydream. The old mare's head was hanging down and her eyes were half closed. It was obvious she was enjoying Angelica's attentions. But there was something sad about her too.

Don't be silly, Ali thought. *She has nothing to be sad about. She's just relaxing.* She carried the water bucket to the mare and held it as Daydream took a sip. Water dribbled from her lips as she pulled away and Ali put the bucket next to the wall.

"What if the intruder sees Daydream isn't in the stable before she goes far enough inside?" asked Ali. "Even if she can't find the light switch in the dark, she'll probably have a flashlight."

Angelica continued to brush Daydream. "Maybe we can trick her. We can tie a string around something heavy and leave it in the straw of Daydream's stall, with the string through the window. When the intruder comes into the stable, you can pull the string from outside. The intruder will hear the sound and think Daydream is lying down in her stall, out of sight behind her door. Then, when the intruder walks toward the stall, I will shut and lock the door behind her."

"That's perfect," said Ali. She smiled. It was so nice to have someone helping her, especially a superhuman somebody with great ideas. "But what about the dog? What if he doesn't go into the stable with her? What if he senses you waiting outside the door?"

"I can go unnoticed by all creatures, if I desire," said Angelica. "My presence will not distract him. But still, he may not follow her inside."

"That would be a big problem," said Ali. "Can you stop him with your light? Or maybe trap him?"

Angelica shook her head. "My light is a healing force. I can use it to surprise but never to harm any creature." She dropped the brush into the grooming kit.

"Well, maybe you can heal him then," said Ali, brightening. "I mean he's so vicious. Maybe your light can help him not be so mad."

"I would not say he is angry. I think he is trained to attack," said Angelica, thoughtfully. "But it is a good idea. Maybe I can communicate with him, tell him he does not have to obey. However, I am not as good at communicating with dogs as horses. He may simply ignore me."

Ali was silent for a few moments. "You've got to reach him somehow. It's the only way to stop him," she finally said.

"I will do the best I can," vowed Angelica. "Come. Let us prepare the stable. We must hurry. It is dark now. She could be here soon."

Ali gave Daydream a quick hug and checked that her rope was well tied. "Now you be quiet, Daydream," she said. "We don't want the intruder knowing you're in here. That would ruin everything." Daydream nickered to her and Ali kissed the mare on her white star. She clicked off the light and securely closed the door when she left.

Ali found a heavy rusted wrench and some twine in the garage and ran back to the stable. She tied it around the wrench in a strong knot, piled some straw in Daydream's stall, laid the wrench on top, and then dropped the end of the twine through the nearest window. "There. Now I'm ready," she said, turning to Angelica.

"Now you must go around the back and wait," said Angelica.

"Where are you going to watch from?" asked Ali as they stepped outside the stable.

Angelica pointed to the shed where Ali kept the grain. "I will wait in there. I can watch through the crack between the door and the building and I can be at the stable door in two or three seconds."

Ali reached inside the stable and clicked the light off. Then she took a deep breath of the brisk night air. This was it. "Good luck, Angelica," she said.

"You too, Ali."

Ali slipped as quietly as she could behind the stable. It was difficult. Her footsteps seemed loud in the stillness of the night. She felt along the back wall until she found the first window. Quickly, she closed and barred the shutters, then continued on toward the second window. Her eager fingers found the twine lying flat against the wall and then she felt for the crack she'd found earlier when it was still light outside. She leaned forward and tried to peer through the crack but couldn't see anything but pitch blackness. She twisted the string nervously around her fingers and waited. And waited.

Seconds slowly ticked by, then minutes. The night seemed abnormally quiet. Not a sound marred the hushed darkness. The two younger horses were far away in the west meadow, a meadow with three different trails on which they could escape. Daydream was silent in her makeshift stall.

Now more than anytime, I wish Scruffy could be here, Ali thought. Unconsciously, her fingers flexed, longing to feel the rough fur on Scruffy's head.

There was a sudden flash of light and a vehicle pulled into the driveway. Ali gasped, then a second later realized it couldn't be the intruder. No, the intruder wouldn't be so bold. She would sneak in on foot. The vehicle stopped and the door opened. Slammed shut. Then the distant murmur of Shelley greeting Peter. And silence.

I'm going to have to go in soon, Ali thought. The minutes continued to tick by like hours. Ali's back was getting sore from bending to peer through the crack but she didn't want to sit down or relax. What if the woman walked in the stable door just after she looked away?

Suddenly she heard something behind her. Every nerve in her body resonated with the sound of stealthy footsteps. The intruder! It couldn't be anyone else.

And she was behind the stable. With Ali!

Ali slowly sank to the ground, trying to keep as silent as possible. Why hadn't she thought of this happening? It made sense. The intruder wasn't going to go marching up to the front door of the stable. No, she would sneak around the back and make sure the coast was clear first.

Ever so slowly, Ali turned her head. The night was cloudy, moonless and starless, but even so, Ali could distinguish a dark shape poised just a car length away. It was all she could do not to scream. Not to run.

But she can't see me! she reminded herself desperately. *Not against the darkness of the stable wall. If I just keep still, she'll keep going.*

But the intruder didn't seem to want to leave. She stood there, still as a statue, listening. Listening. The sound of Ali's heart seemed to swell and fill the night. She was sure the intruder would hear the rapid beat. Sweat beaded her forehead as she stared at the figure, waiting for the black head to turn toward her. Waiting for the sinister form to call the dog to attack. When she couldn't stand the suspense anymore, Ali squeezed her eyes shut.

Be calm, she commanded herself. *Think of Daydream. Think of Scruffy.*

A soft tread and Ali's eyes popped open. The shadow crept around the side of the stable. Relief swept through Ali and she sucked a deep breath into her lungs. She cautiously rose to her feet and peered through the crack again. The intruder wasn't at the door yet.

A strange feeling niggled at Ali's mind. She looked over her shoulder, her heart in her throat. Nothing! But still, she felt as if she was being watched. Was it the dog? Was he lurking in the darkness behind her, observing her every move? Waiting to attack?

There was a soft scuffing sound from inside the stable and Ali forced herself to ignore the strange feeling. She peered through the crack again. The lighting in the stable had changed. It wasn't so dark. She thought she could see the faint outline of the open doorway. With trembling hands, she tugged on the string. The wrench slid in the straw. She heard a quick intake of breath. The sound had startled the intruder.

"Margot?"

The voice *was* familiar. *No, it can't be,* thought Ali. *It can't be her!*

Suddenly the door slammed. The intruder screamed. Ali's pulse raced as she threw her arms up and shoved the shutters shut. She flipped the bar across the strong wood and collapsed against the back wall of the stable, her heart beating like crazy. They had her! They had caught the intruder!

The feeling of being watched still troubled Ali as she hurried around the side of the stable. At the corner she glanced behind her. Her eyes searched the night but she could see nothing. If the dog was out there, he wasn't coming forward.

Angelica met her when she turned the corner of the stable. "It's Maddie," she said.

Ali had recognized Maddie's voice the second she'd heard it. She just hadn't wanted to believe it. "I know," she said.

"Are you all right?" asked Angelica.

"Mom will be so upset. And I am too," she admitted. "Maddie's irritating sometimes, but she's our friend. At least I thought she was." She paused. "How am I going to tell Mom?"

"Ali? Is that you?" Maddie's panicky voice came from the other side of the door. "Ali? Ali! You've got to let me out."

Ali looked at Angelica. Let her out? Why would they let her out? She must be nuts to think they'd just open the door.

"Ali, I know it looks suspicious, but you have to believe me," pleaded Maddie. "I had nothing to do with

Rhythm and Crystal's disappearance. Or with the dog attacking Scruffy. I swear."

"I don't believe you," Ali replied. Here Maddie was, trying to weasel out of being caught.

"Please, Ali," Maddie continued to beg. "You have to let me out. Before it's too late."

Ali and Angelica looked at each other. "She's trying to trick us," Ali whispered. Then she added, loud enough for Maddie to hear her, "Why did you do it, Maddie? I thought you were our friend. How could you be so sneaky and cruel and nasty and horrible and... " Ali's voice faded away. She couldn't think of any words strong enough to describe Maddie's betrayal.

"Oh Ali, I would never hurt you. Or your mom. Shelley's my best friend and I've known you since the day you were born. How could you think I'd do such a horrible thing as hurt poor Daydream?"

Ali was suddenly uncertain. "She sounds like she really means what she says," she whispered to Angelica.

As if she knew there was a tiny bit of hope, Maddie redoubled her pleas. "I would never *ever* do anything to hurt you or your mom. You've got to believe me. I didn't come here to harm anyone."

"Why *are* you here then?" asked Ali.

There was no reply.

"Maddie?"

"I can't tell you why. I'm sorry Ali." The voice was firm.

"Then I have to tell Mom and Peter everything that's been happening," said Ali. "Maybe you'll explain it to them."

"No! Please Ali. Please don't tell them." Maddie sounded like she was about to cry.

"Then tell me the truth. Tell me why you're here, if it's not to hurt Daydream."

There was a long silence, then, "I... I can't."

Ali didn't know what to do. She would rather solve the mystery without her mom and Peter knowing about it. It would be easier for everyone that way. But Maddie was leaving her no choice.

She felt Angelica's hand on her shoulder. "Let me try," whispered the golden girl. When Ali nodded, she said, "Maddie?"

"Who's that?"

"Do you not recognize my voice?"

"Angelica?"

Ali gasped. Angelica and Maddie knew each other?

"You do remember," Angelica said gently. "I helped you and your mare, Scarlett, many years ago."

"I'll never forget. You saved Scarlett's life," said Maddie, her voice a little more relaxed. "You've come to help Daydream and the others, haven't you?"

"Yes, and we need you to tell us the truth. I cannot believe you would hurt Ali and the horses. But I am not wrong in saying you know who *does* want to hurt them, am I?"

A tiny whisper. "No."

"Then tell us."

"I can't. Really, Angelica, I can't tell anyone. But you have to let me go. I have to protect Daydream. Ali said Daydream would be in the stable tonight and I knew I had to do something to save her. You see I'm the only one who can stop... *her*. Angelica, Ali, you have to open the door."

"You have to tell us who you're protecting Daydream from first," said Ali, unable to keep quiet any longer.

"Maddie? Maddie, is that you?" The voice came from behind them, then a giggle. A high-pitched, unnatural giggle that sent shivers up Ali's spine.

Ali and Angelica spun around to see a dark shape walk toward them, a giant dog hulking at its side.

Ali

"Oh Margot! Yes, it's me, Maddie. Please, please, don't run away! I have to talk to you! Ali, Angelica, let me out!" Maddie yelled. Her fists pounded on the sturdy wooden door. "Margot, just wait until I get out! Please!"

A beam of light flashed from the woman's hand and brightened the stable door. "Why do you have Maddie locked away?" The voice was puzzled.

"Please Ali, let me out," Maddie begged.

The woman giggled again. "How does it feel, Maddie? Being locked away. Just like you did to me. After the accident. The accident. Do you like it? Like it?"

Ali looked at Angelica in confusion.

The light moved on to Angelica and the woman's voice faltered for a moment. "I know you. I think. Think. You're that alien, that weird girl, the one who came to fix Maddie's horse. That big smelly horse of Maddie's." A low laugh tumbled toward them and Ali shuddered. "Smelly Scarlett. Scarlett smells." The flashlight swept back to the stable door. "Do you want me to let you out, Maddie?"

"Yes, Margot, please."

"No, no, no. I can't. I don't have the key." Another high-pitched laugh. "The key. The key. I stole the key and got away, Maddie. But then I threw it away. Sorry. Sorry."

Angelica interrupted her with a gentle voice. "Margot, why do you want to hurt the horses?"

"What do you mean?" The light flashed back to Angelica's face. "I don't hurt them. I help them. I stop their pain. I love them." She sounded like a small child trying to explain to her mom why she'd cut her Barbie's hair, proud of what she'd done but sad her mom was disappointed in her. She shifted in the darkness. "A favour. Favour. Understand? I'm doing them a favour. That one today? He was in pain. I stopped his pain. He's happy now."

"Margot, why did you come here?" Angelica tried again. With one hand she motioned to Ali to move closer to the stable door. "Why did you come to Anela Ranch?"

"Don't you know? I live here. My home this is. This is my home. Home. Didn't you know?"

Maddie's voice came through the stable door. "She's my sister, Angelica." She sounded like she was crying. "My sister."

"Sisters," whispered Ali. Suddenly it all made sense. That's why Daydream found the intruder familiar, even though she didn't know her. That's why Ali almost recognized her when Daydream tried to communicate with her and why Peter mistook Margot for Maddie. She looked more closely at Margot's face, barely illuminated by the flashlight she held. "You're twins," she said in shock. "Identical twins."

The light jumped toward Ali for the first time.

"You!" Margot screamed. "Shelley! Thief! Murderer!"

Ali felt a wave of revulsion rush through her. The woman's voice was poisoned with hatred.

Angelica stepped forward. "No, no, Margot. She is not Shelley. Her name is Ali." Her voice was soothing, but it seemed to have no effect.

"She's tricking you! She dyed her hair. It's Shelley! It's her!"

Ali reached out and her fingers searched for the lock. If she could set Maddie free, Maddie might be able to talk some sense into her sister. The lock clicked and Ali's hand moved to the doorknob.

"You hurt me, Shelley! You killed Daddy! Daddy!" Margot screamed. "Wolf!" The dog looked at Margot with terrified eyes. "Get them, Wolf! Attack!"

The black dog glowered at Ali and Angelica for a millisecond, then leapt forward with a snarl.

"No!" yelled Angelica. Light arched from her hands in the same instant the door to the stable burst open. Maddie stood there for an instant, her hair in disarray and her face wet with tears, then she pulled Ali into her arms to protect her.

Angelica's light surrounded Wolf in a burst of brightness and he skidded to a stop. He looked nervously behind him but his mistress was gone. What did she want him to do now? Attack the light creature? Or the girl standing behind her? Or the woman who looked and smelled similar to his mistress?

As he stood, wide-eyed, Angelica's light flowed softer and more tender. It wove around the dog in an intricate dance, creating beautiful loops and graceful designs. Wolf growled and snapped as a filament of light touched his jaw. The light swept away from the dog's muzzle and Wolf looked at Angelica and whined.

"What's she doing?" Maddie asked Ali, her voice filled with awe. Her arms fell to her side.

Ali was quiet for a moment as she watched another filament touch the dog's forehead. This time Wolf shut his eyes. Then the music started, a melody as buoyant as a song slipped inside the wind, as elemental as waves falling silken on moonlit beaches. Ali closed her eyes and the strange music vibrated through her mind and pulsed in time with her heart.

"She's trying to communicate with him," she whispered to Maddie as quietly as she could. She didn't want to interrupt the magic of the song. "Angelica is telling him he needs to make his own decisions, not just follow orders. And that he doesn't have to be frightened of his owner anymore."

"Ali, look," whispered Maddie.

Ali opened her eyes and gasped. The light was skipping to the cadence of the music. And it was more than white light now. Strains of blue wove between red and yellow, violet and green. All the colors of the rainbow were flowing around and through one another in a glorious dance of light. Wolf lay in the center of the circle, his adoring eyes fastened on Angelica.

Ali smiled. Angelica could do anything. She was truly amazing. Ali could feel the soothing calmness of Angelica's light herself. The power of it was throbbing through the air, surrounding her. Beside Ali, Maddie's stance relaxed even more.

We can't relax too much, Ali reminded herself. *Margot's still out there.* But still, she couldn't shake the feeling of well being that surrounded her as she watched Wolf become gentle before her eyes. He didn't look like a brute anymore. He was just an ordinary dog. What had it taken to turn him into such a monster? How cruel had Margot been to him? Or was he just frightened of her insanity?

"Maddie?" whispered Ali. "What happened to Margot? Was she always like that?"

"No, Ali. She was wonderful while we were growing up. I loved her more than anyone. I still do love her, but it's different now."

"Why does she hate my mom so much?"

"It's complicated. Our father was a gambler. He owed a lot of money to a lot of bad people, money that he couldn't pay. So he sold the ranch to your grandparents and Shelley inherited it when they died."

"So Margot hates my mom because we live here?"

"Yes, but there's more to it than that."

Maddie was silent for so long that Ali pulled her gaze from the light. Fresh tears streamed down Maddie's face. "You don't have to tell me," Ali said gently.

"I want to. You deserve to know, after all you've been through," said Maddie and took a deep breath. "There was an accident, a car accident, a month after Dad sold the ranch to your grandparents. Dad was killed in the crash and Margot was with him. She hit her head. At first we thought she was going to be okay, but then... " She stopped to wipe the tears from her eyes. "Then she started acting strange. Obsessing about the ranch. Somehow the sale of the ranch, the crash, and Dad's death all meshed together in her mind. She began saying your family had murdered Dad. And she started doing other things too, self-destructive things. Finally, Mom had to send her to an institution and then, when Mom passed on, I became Margot's legal guardian."

She paused again and together the two of them watched the light frolic around the dog. Finally Maddie continued. "For years I told her I would get her out of there as soon as I could. But when I became her legal guardian, I talked to the doctors and I realized Mom had been right. Margot was too sick to be out in the world. I had to protect her, from herself." Tears were strong in Maddie's voice. "I visited her every Sunday, Ali, and every time she cried and begged me to take her away. It was so horrible."

"Won't she ever get well?"

"Who knows? Maybe someday. Miracles can happen," said Maddie. She sighed. "About three weeks ago her doctor phoned me. Margot had tricked one of the night nurses and escaped. We discovered she'd withdrawn a lot of money from her bank account, the one holding the insurance money from the accident, and that was the last we heard of her. It was as if she'd disappeared off the face of the earth, until this morning. When you asked me why I came over last night, I suddenly realized she was here, somewhere. And that she was behind the attack on Scruffy."

"She's been here for a while," admitted Ali. "I didn't say anything because I was afraid Mom would sell, but Margot's been sabotaging things around the ranch. And then lately, she's been trying to hurt the horses."

"I'm sorry about your horses, Ali." Maddie's voice cracked.

"Don't worry," whispered Ali. "They're safe. Thanks to Angelica."

Maddie took a deep, trembling breath and exhaled slowly. "I'm so glad she was here to help you."

"Maddie, I'm sorry I suspected you," whispered Ali.

"It's okay, Ali. I would have done the same in your place. How could you have known?" She reached out and took Ali's hand in hers, and together they watched the dancing tendrils before them fade. Angelica was almost finished weaving her magic.

Wolf, you finally understand we are not like her. I can feel your acceptance. And your relief. You see we will not hurt you. But do you understand how your actions forced pain upon other living creatures? The same pain that was forced upon you by your mistress? It is a circle that must end here.

The dog you attacked yesterday did not hate you. The two humans here, they do not hate you. None wish to cause you harm. So let me ask you, why do you wish to hurt them?

Another, full of fury and madness, commanded it, that is true. And you are afraid of her. But is that reason enough for you now?

No? I am glad.

The woman stopped when she was a safe distance away, hidden by the welcome cloak of night. She turned and hunkered down. They had Wolf. She could see him clearly, trapped in the alien's light. She longed to call him away, but she couldn't let them know where she was.

"She's hurting him. Hurting him," she muttered. "He wants me to save him." Tears sprang from her eyes as she thought of how Wolf was being tortured, of how cruel and heartless they were, trapping him in the light. It was all Shelley's fault. Anger coursed through her body and she heard a growl. When she realized the sound was coming from her own mouth, she didn't stop. Instead she formed the guttural noise into words.

"I'll avenge you, Wolf," she snarled. "I'll avenge both of us. Both of us. They can't send us back to that place. I won't let them. No. No."

She crept forward, low to the ground.

As the last tendril of light disappeared into nothingness, the dog whined and crept toward Angelica. The golden girl sank to her knees and held her hand out toward him. "Come, Wolf," she whispered. The dog slunk the rest of the way and cowered before her. "Do not worry, Wolf. You are not in trouble." Her hand stroked the dog's massive head. "We will not hurt you as Margot did. We will care for you." She looked up at Ali and Maddie. "Maddie, will you take him? Will you keep him safe and treat him with kindness and love?"

Maddie hesitated. "But he's an attack dog, Angelica. A killer," she said.

"No longer," said Angelica. "Wolf has given his vow to never harm any creature. But he is alone in the world now. He does not want to be with Margot. He is afraid of her. And his previous owner was cruel to him. He beat Wolf many times. Wolf needs someone to care for him."

Maddie nodded. "Okay, Angelica. Because I trust you, I'll give him a home. But I don't want to call him Wolf. It's a name for a mean dog and I don't like it. How about Amigo?"

Angelica's hand glowed a warm light on the top of Wolf's head. He whined and rolled his eyes toward Maddie. Then Angelica whispered in his ear. When the glow died, Angelica motioned Maddie forward.

"He will answer to Amigo," she said in a weak voice.

While Maddie bent and tentatively patted Amigo on the head, Angelica looked at Ali. "I guess I can communicate with dogs better than I thought," she said. A wan smile touched her face.

"Is something wrong, Angelica?" asked Ali, worried by the weariness in the girl's voice. She went to the door to the stable and reached inside to turn on the light. The bright bulb spilled vibrant light through the doorway and onto the four beings. Amigo stood beside Maddie, looking at her with hopeful eyes. But Angelica was still sitting on the ground, her hair glimmered a faint silver in the bright light.

"I am weak, that is all. The energy it took to communicate with Amigo was great and I have little left."

"What do we do now?" asked Maddie.

Ali thought for a moment. "I'll go get Daydream," she said, remembering how Crystal and Rhythm's tears had healed Angelica the last time.

"What? Why?"

"There's no time to explain," said Ali. "You need to find Margot. You can use Wolf... uh, Amigo, to track her. Angelica and I will catch up to you in a few minutes, but we can't let Margot get too much of a head start."

"Come, Amigo," Maddie said tentatively and turned in the direction Margot had gone. The big black dog padded away at her side, his head up and ears forward.

Ali knelt beside Angelica. "I'll be back in a minute," she said. "It'll be easier to bring Daydream to you."

Angelica nodded and Ali noticed that the silver in her hair had almost faded to white, and that Angelica's energy seemed to be leaving with the last of the color. "I'll be right back," she repeated and hurried into the darkness.

She was halfway to the garden shed when the feeling of being watched returned. Ali looked behind her to see Angelica lying in the pool of light. Maddie was long gone. Then she heard someone exhale. Margot! She was close by, hidden in the night. Fear zapped down Ali's spine and it was all she could do to calmly turn and keep walking, pretending she hadn't heard a thing. If Margot wanted to attack her, she would have done it already. No, she was waiting for something – or someone – else.

Ali walked to the garden shed, unlatched the door, and ducked inside. She pulled the door shut behind her, leaving it open just enough to peer through. Daydream nickered in greeting behind her.

"Shhh," whispered Ali, her eyes watching for movement in the dark. *She could be right next to me,* she realized. *It's so dark I can hardly see anything.*

Then Ali saw her, creeping low to the ground toward Angelica. *She's stalking Angelica. But why?* The dark form moved like liquid night against the brightness spilling from the stable, stealing closer and closer to her unwary prey. It was then that Ali noticed that Angelica's hair, almost white in her weakness, was the same color as Ali's mom's – white blonde – and she understood. Margot thought Angelica was Shelley. *And she hates my mom more than anything.* The thought made Ali feel sick. How was she going to warn Angelica?

But there was no need. The exhausted girl raised her hand in a feeble greeting. "Hello, Margot," she said.

And Margot stepped into the light. "Shelley, Shelley," she hissed. "Do you a favour? A favour?"

Rage! Power! Hate!
  Revenge! Glorious revenge! At last.
  "You hurt me. Hurt me. Over and over, you hurt me. And now you hurt Wolf too. A favour for Wolf. For me. For Daddy. No hurting us anymore. Not anymore. I won't let you. Stop you, I will. Stop you forever. And ever."

Ali exploded from the shed, her blood roaring in her ears. She had to stop Margot. She had to save Angelica. Somehow!

Daydream's piercing neigh brought her back to her senses. She wasn't strong enough to save Angelica, not from Margot who probably had the super-human strength that insanity often lent to people. And if Ali wasn't stronger, she would have to be smarter.

She ran back to the garden shed, clicked on the light and raced to Daydream's stall. With nimble fingers, she untied the lead rope, then leapt onto the mare's back. She leaned forward and Daydream surged ahead. The mare might be old, but she would still be stronger than Margot.

Suddenly Ali pulled Daydream back. A glimmer of silver had caught her eye. *Mom's throw net. That's it!* She circled Daydream and reached for the net hanging on the wall, lifting it cleanly from the high hook. She tossed it over her shoulders the way her mom had taught her.

"Let's go, girl." She urged the already panting mare forward with her heels. "You can do this. I know you can. If you think you're too tired, just remember

141

Angelica can heal you after, just like she did with Rhythm."

Daydream burst from the stable with Ali low on her back, the net flaring behind her like a silver cape. The mare's ears were pinned back and her nose jutted forward as she trotted toward Margot and Angelica. Angelica had rallied herself enough to rise to her knees and Margot paced around her, her hair dishevelled and eyes glazed. She ground her teeth together in hatred.

"Stop!" Ali screamed and Margot looked up. She was almost there now, and Daydream was closing fast. For a moment Margot looked confused, then her burning eyes dropped back to Angelica. She lunged forward.

Daydream broke into a rough gallop and ran straight toward the struggling pair. Ali screamed as Margot's fists went up and down, up and down. The sound of flesh hitting flesh almost made her sick. "No!" she screamed. "No!"

Daydream didn't stop when she reached Margot and Angelica. Instead, she leapt over the exhausted girl's body and her hooves caught Margot on the shoulder, sending the woman flying. Within a second, Ali was on the ground, standing between the crazed woman and Angelica.

"Stay back," she threatened. "Leave her alone."

Margot straightened in front of Ali. "You can't stop me. Stop me," she hissed.

Ali didn't know where she was finding the courage to face the deranged woman. She ached to see if Angelica was all right but she knew she couldn't turn her back on Margot. Her hands grasped the net and she slid it off her shoulder.

Margot stepped forward, murder smouldering in her eyes. *"You're Shelley!"* she shrieked and reached into her pocket. A second later, she flipped open a small penknife. Her crazed eyes glistened as she stalked toward Ali.

Ali threw the net. It floated into the air, a perfect, lacy circle and dropped over Margot's body, wrapping around her. Margot jerked her knife hand close to her side, protecting it. Then, with her eyes locked on Ali, she moved the knife in her hand so the blade was at a different angle. She glared through the weave of the net as she hacked at the fibres.

Ali didn't hesitate. She knew this would be her only chance. She ran at the woman with her head lowered and heard a loud "oof" – Margot was down. The knife slashed out as Ali jumped back, but the net hindered the woman's movements. Ali was on her feet just in time to see the net tangle around the blade, around the woman's body and head – and to see her lose her grip on the knife. It landed at her feet.

Ali leapt for the blade in the same instant Margot tumbled forward, scrambling for the curved handle. Overeager fingers sent the knife skittering across the ground, away from them both. The woman grabbed at Ali, and for a moment she had her by her jacket, but again the net affected her grip.

Ali pulled away, jumped to her feet, and glared down at Margot with gritted teeth. Anger hummed through her body and she wanted to scream and scream with rage. This woman had almost killed Rhythm and Scruffy. She wanted to kill Ali's mother. Ali wanted to slam against her again and again. Hit her over and over. Somehow expend the incredible fury that was

143

almost overwhelming her. But she couldn't do it. Even through her rage, she knew it wouldn't be right. Instead, she stood frozen and watched Margot climb to her feet. The woman staggered toward the blade, sobbed and fell again, her net wrapped hand almost within reach of the knife.

As quickly as it had come, Ali's rage dissipated. Margot whimpered like a caged beast as her fingers closed around her prize but Ali could only look at her with pity. "Margot," she whispered. "You're not going to win." She held her hand out. "Give me the knife."

Margot sniffled in reply.

"Please Margot, please give me the knife," said Ali.

"Stay away! Stay away! Don't kill me too!"

Behind Margot, Ali saw Angelica push herself up with her arms. The girl reached up and stroked Daydream's tear streaked face, then kissed her greying muzzle. She entwined her fingers in the mare's mane and pulled herself to her feet.

"She thinks we're going to kill her," Ali whispered.

"She needs our help, Ali."

Terror flashed into Margot's eyes as she jerked her head around to see Angelica. Angelica smiled softly at Margot and stepped toward her. She stopped when Margot cringed beneath the net. Then suddenly she looked into the darkness behind Ali. And Ali heard it too. Running footsteps.

"You must help her, if you can," Angelica whispered. Then she put her finger to her lips and Ali nodded to the older girl. She wouldn't say a word. Without another sound, Angelica faded into the night.

Shelley and Peter burst into the stable's light.

"What? Maddie, Ali, what are you doing?" said Ali's mom, confused. She took a quick step back when Margot looked at her, hatred blazing from her eyes. "Margot! What are you doing here?" Shelley's voice was a horrified whisper.

The next thing Ali knew, Maddie and Amigo were there too. When Maddie saw Margot wrapped in the net, she looked at Ali with respect, then strode forward and snatched the knife from her sister's hand.

More confusion. So many explanations. Daydream to check. The police and Margo's hospital to call. Her mom half hysterical when Ali told her what had been happening. And Peter calming Shelley. Holding her. Helping her understand that Ali really was okay.

Peter and Maddie were the last to leave. By the time Peter finally pulled his truck out of the driveway, taking Maddie and Amigo with him, Ali was exhausted. She could hardly believe it was all over. No more intruder. No more maliciousness. Just her and her mom, the horses and Scruffy, at home on Anela Ranch. Everything was finally back the way it should be.

After Peter's headlights faded into the night, Ali turned to her mom. "I'm going to go check on Daydream one more time," she said.

"Do you want me to come with you?" asked Shelley.

"No, I'll just be a couple minutes." Ali had no desire to stay longer. Her muscles ached and she could almost hear her bed calling her. She just wanted to double check that Daydream was okay after her ordeal.

The mare greeted her with a low whinny. "Hello, magical wild moonflower horse," said Ali when she saw Daydream's white star floating in the darkness of the stable. She flipped on the light.

Angelica stood in the mare's stall, slowly moving the brush across Daydream's side. She smiled at Ali. "I was hoping you would come to see Daydream again tonight," she said.

"Are you really okay, Angelica?" asked Ali, hurrying to Daydream's stall. "Margot didn't hurt you too much did she?"

"I am perfectly fine," said Angelica. "And do not worry. Daydream is fine as well."

"I am so relieved." Ali ran her fingers through Daydream's dark forelock. "What a strange night. I never would have guessed that Maddie had a twin sister. And one so crazy. Maddie always seemed so normal."

"She was nice as a girl too. You would have liked her." Angelica moved to Daydream's left side and continued to brush her.

Ali smiled. It seemed so weird to imagine her mother's best friend as a young girl.

"Ali, I have something for you," said Angelica, stepping to the stall door. Suddenly, her hair began to glow and swirl in a nonexistent wind. Angelica smiled as she twined a single hair around her index finger and tugged. She cupped the golden strand in her hands. "Hold your hand out."

Angelica dropped the hair onto Ali's palm – but it was no longer a hair. A delicate golden chain lay in her hand. Ali gasped and lifted it to see it better. It chimed gently and a warm tingle spread through her fingers.

"Let me," said Angelica, taking it from her. She held the necklace in two hands and, reaching over the stall door, slipped it over Ali's head. "If you ever need me, Ali, just touch the necklace and call my name. The necklace will relay your message."

"Thank you, Angelica," said Ali, in awe. "It's amazing. So beautiful. And thank you for saving the horses and Scruffy and me. And for healing Rhythm. And Amigo too. How can we ever pay you back?"

"You have. You saved me from Margot. I thank you for that, you and your lovely Daydream." Her fingers lingered over the mare's face, then she leaned forward and whispered in the mare's ear.

Ali felt tears come to her eyes as she watched. Angelica was saying goodbye. Daydream nuzzled her and nickered, then Angelica stepped away. She slipped from the stall. "Do you want to come with me as I say goodbye to the others?" she asked Ali.

"I wish I could," said Ali. "But I promised Mom I'd be back in a minute. She's had a pretty rough night."

"You are a good daughter, Ali," said Angelica. "I will say goodbye here then." She pulled Ali into a hug, then slowly released her.

"Goodbye," she whispered. Then she slipped out the stable door, and was gone.

147

*Crystal! Rhythm! There you are! Rejoice my loved
ones. All is well. The intruder has been taken away.
Your dam, the lovely Daydream, is well, as are Ali and
her mother.*

*Come, I will tell you of it. Then we must say goodbye.
Another needs me soon. Roland. His leg was broken in
a race and his owner has put a cast on it. Roland is
frightened and impatient. He struggles against the
ropes and slings that are designed to help him. He does
not understand he needs to be still until his leg mends.
I will go to him and comfort him. Teach him. But we
have a few minutes until his owner leaves the stable.*

*First, let me tell you how brave Daydream and Ali
were, and then let us run together! Unfettered and free!*

Ali skipped along the path to the beach, the net over her shoulders and Daydream walking sedately behind. It had been a wonderful week. Good things just kept on happening. Scruffy was hobbling about, nosing into corners and making sure everything was shipshape again. Crystal and Rhythm were healthy and happy – well, Rhythm wasn't just happy; he was ecstatic! He ran everywhere he went, which irritated Crystal so much that she kept laying her ears back at him. And Ali's mom had promised she would never sell the ranch.

And there was even more good news. Maddie had come over the night before to tell them of the new treatment Margot's doctors had started. Maddie had positively gushed with hopefulness and, for the first time in a long time, Ali didn't find her too irritating. There was even good news at school – the kids hadn't teased Ali since her friend, Sarah, told them all about Ali capturing Margot.

"First I'm the freaky horse lover and now I'm the tough kid in school. Boy, are they ever clueless!" Ali said and spun around, the net swinging wide behind her. The little weights around its edge clacked together and she laughed. It was a sun-drenched Saturday afternoon and the world was perfect. Even the time her mom and Peter were spending together didn't bother her too much. In fact, Peter was getting to be kind of fun.

But the best thing of all was that Daydream seemed just fine after her experiences the weekend before. Ali smiled and waited for the old mare to catch up with her, then the two of them walked on together, side by side.

When they got to the beach, Ali pushed her mother's small boat from above the high tide line to the edge of the water. "You wait here, Daydream. I want to surprise Mom with a nice big fish. Don't worry. I promise I won't go out of the bay."

Ali threw the net on the seat of the skiff and was about to jump in when she hesitated. She turned back to Daydream and lifted the necklace from around her neck. "Just in case I decide to go swimming," she said to the mare. "I don't want to lose it." She braided the necklace into Daydream's mane, then pushed the boat into the gentle waves and leapt inside. With her back to the open ocean, she rowed toward the outer rocks that tumbled from the end of the beach far out into the water.

In the center of the bay, she stopped. The turquoise blue water was like a fluid jewel around her, the black beach behind her like obsidian. Lush vegetation framed the black expanse and glowed vibrant green against the brilliant sky. Ali took a deep breath, pulled the oars inside the boat, lay back on the seat, and put her feet up. The sun was hot on her face and she threw her hand across her forehead to shade her eyes. With her head turned to the side, she watched Daydream wander along the edge of the beach. The mare reached a pile of seaweed and stopped to sniff it. Ali closed her eyes. The water sloshed and splashed against the side of the small craft as it bobbed in the gentle waves.

It's almost like music, thought Ali. *I could go to sleep out here. What am I talking about? I have gone to sleep in the skiff before.* She remembered the particularly wicked sunburn she'd gotten. Was that only last summer? It seemed so long ago. She drew a deep breath of sea air and stretched her arms above her head, then brought them down to rest across her stomach.

Where's Angelica now? Ali wondered. *What horse is she helping?* She smiled thinking of her friend and murmured out loud, "Angelica, will I ever see you again?"

The boat was rolling a little more heavily now. Ali opened her eyes. The sky was perfect above her. So peaceful. So clear and calm. Maybe she should rouse herself and go for a swim in her safe little bay. The water would be refreshingly cool after this heat. She could always go fishing later.

Automatically, her eyes moved to the beach to find Daydream. The mare was looking out to the open sea. And she seemed farther away. A *lot* farther away. Ali drew another deep breath and her eyes slid to the rocks at the edge of the beach, the ones that should have been beside her. But they weren't there.

She sat up, making the little boat loll heavily in her haste. Her feet splashed into the bottom of the boat. Water in the boat? The boat was leaking?

But it was fine last time I used it, Ali remembered, unable to accept the fact it had filled with water so quickly. She could feel the flow racing into the boat almost beneath her heels and looked closer. A number of perfectly round holes had been drilled in the bottom.

What? How did that happen? How am I going to get the boat back before it sinks? Ali looked up. The rocks were already farther away. The boat was moving fast, directly away from the shore. She was being swept out to sea!

Ali jerked the oars into place and rowed with all her might. She had to get close to the rocks before the boat went down. But the rocks only grew more and more distant. Breathing heavily, Ali shook her head in frustration. What was happening? The water sloshed against her ankles, reminding her she didn't have much time. The boat was already low in the water.

That's it! she suddenly realized. *The boat is low in the water and the undercurrents have caught it.* The thought sent a tremor of fear down her spine. Her mom was always warning her not to leave the shelter of their bay. The undercurrents outside it were deadly. They would carry her far from the beach within minutes. Carry her out to sea. And then the boat would sink.

And I didn't wear a lifejacket. Mom told me to remember and I totally forgot. What an idiot I am!

Daydream was the only one who could hear her call for help. Ali's hand shot to her neck. The necklace! She almost cried when she remembered braiding it into Daydream's mane.

Why did I do that? Oh Angelica, if only you could hear me. I need you! Then the answer came to her. Daydream could summon Angelica. She didn't need a necklace. "Daydream!" Ali shrieked. The mare's head shot up. "Daydream, get help! Call Angelica!"

Daydream didn't hesitate. She stepped into the water and sloshed toward Ali.

"No!" screamed Ali. "Stay, Daydream! Just call Angelica! Let *her* save me!" She stood in the boat and waved her hands. But the mare kept coming.

Suddenly the boat rocked to the side and Ali plunged into the frothing ocean. The water closed over her head and she could feel the powerful tug of the current sweeping her away. She struggled toward the surface with all her might. When she broke through, she gulped the sweet air. The current had pulled her even farther. Now the boat was between her and the shore.

I have to keep as close to the surface as I can, she realized. *Otherwise the undertow will take me away much faster.* She felt the sting of salt water in her eyes. *But Daydream can't stay near the surface! She'll be swept out to sea if she comes out this far.*

The briny water splashed into her mouth and she choked. Gagged. Then she swam toward shore. The boat swept past her, out to sea.

Ali was too close to the water's surface now to see Daydream's dark head above the waves and could only hope that when the mare didn't see her, she would turn back to the safety of the beach.

Ali swam and swam and swam, until her muscles burned and she was gasping for breath. The rocks were a little closer. Just a little. For a moment, Ali relaxed and looked back. The boat was gone. She didn't know if it had sunk altogether or had been swept completely out of sight, but it didn't matter. Whatever had happened to it, she would suffer the same fate if she didn't make it to shore soon. Ali redoubled her efforts though her arms and legs felt like lead weights.

She was aware of the exact moment she began to lose ground and despair punctured the miniscule bit of strength she had left. She wasn't strong enough, wasn't tough enough, to make it to shore. She would be swept out to sea and drowned. Her mother would never know what happened to her. Ali would never see Daydream or Rhythm or Crystal or Scruffy again. For the first time ever, Ali was glad Peter was with Shelley. He would comfort her. He would take care of her.

Ali rolled onto her back. She might as well spend the last bit of her strength in staying afloat rather than fighting to reach some rocks she would never reach anyway.

Then she heard breathing. Harsh, heavy breathing. She flipped over in the water to face the sound. Daydream! The mare hadn't turned back! A wave of relief and sadness swept over Ali. Daydream would save her, if she could. But was *she* strong enough?

Then Daydream was beside her. Ali grabbed the mare's mane and the dark horse swam in a circle, then headed for the closest land, the black rocks. Ali kicked as hard as she could, trying to be as little a burden as possible. Maybe Daydream was strong enough to save them. Maybe she was a good enough swimmer.

Within a few minutes, Ali could tell she was. The rocks were coming closer. So, so slowly, but they *were* coming closer. Daydream's breathing was growing louder. Harsher. The mare looked back at Ali and the girl shuddered. She didn't like the glazed look in Daydream's eyes. Somehow she forced her exhausted legs to kick harder.

"You can do it, Daydream," she gasped. "I know you can. You have to."

Suddenly, Ali remembered the necklace. With numb fingers she searched Daydream's mane. No glint of gold. No magical tingle. The necklace was gone.

The mare quivered under Ali's hand and she looked up to see that they were losing ground. "No," she moaned. "Oh, Daydream."

"Take my hand, Ali. I will help you to the rocks." Ali turned her head to see Angelica treading water beside her, her hand outstretched and her eyes glowing with power. For a moment, Ali hesitated. She didn't want to leave Daydream. *But she'll get to shore easier if she doesn't have to drag me*, she realized and reached for Angelica's offered hand.

Angelica was a powerful swimmer, much stronger than Ali, and they moved quickly toward the rocks. Ali couldn't do anything to help though she tried, but her legs and arms had nothing left to give. Nothing at all.

When she felt the first of the rough lava rocks beneath her feet, Ali knew she was safe. Angelica helped her up onto the first of the rocks and Ali collapsed. She coughed and gasped for breath, the waves brushing against her toes. Angelica waited, her hand on Ali's shoulder.

"You will be all right now?" she finally asked.

Ali nodded. "Daydream," she gasped. "Is she at the beach yet?"

Angelica's eyes swept out to sea and Ali turned her head. Daydream wasn't still out there. Was she?

Then Ali saw the dark speck far out on the ocean. She struggled to her feet. "Daydream!" she screamed, her hands cupped around her mouth. Daydream was so far away, Ali couldn't even see the white star on her forehead. She turned to Angelica, her hands clasped in front of her. "Angelica, do something. Save her," she begged. "Please. Please!"

Angelica's eyes filled with tears as she shook her head. "There is nothing I can do."

"No!" Ali spun back to see Daydream's head still above the waves. For a moment longer, the mare struggled to stay afloat, to somehow make it to shore. Then she slipped beneath the waves. The waters closed over her head without a ripple and Ali screamed. Daydream was gone.

Ali collapsed on the rock, her face in her hands. She couldn't accept it. Daydream couldn't be gone. Not really. Wild eyed, she looked out at the waves again. No dark head above the water. She looked toward the beach. No Daydream.

But how can that be? Daydream can't leave me! In her mind, Ali imagined the mare swimming to the surface, pulling toward the beach with powerful strokes. Her eyes searched the water again. *Please, Daydream, please!* But there was nothing.

The emotional storm in Ali's heart exploded to the surface. She sobbed like she had never sobbed before. Great racking moans that tore at her heart and made her sick to her stomach. Her fingers tingled and her entire body shook with violent tremors. And always Angelica's arms were around her, holding her. Trying uselessly to comfort her.

Ali felt years older when she finally looked up with swollen, tear-filled eyes. Angelica was still there, rubbing her back. Her golden tresses looked like burnished metal in the evening light. "She saved me, Angelica," Ali whispered, her voice cracking with emotion. "Daydream saved me."

"Yes," whispered Angelica. "She loves you."

"It's my fault she… " Ali shut her mouth tightly. She couldn't say that word.

"Ali, no!" Angelica protested. "Her death is not your fault. Do not say that."

"But if I hadn't gotten in the boat, or if I was watching instead of just lying back on the seat, or if I'd noticed it was leaking sooner, she might still be here."

"The boat was leaking, Ali?" asked Angelica. Her voice had a strange edge to it.

"There were holes in it. I saw them. It looked like they'd been made with a drill." She gasped. "Margot. Margot drilled a hole in Mom's boat." Her words choked to a stop and she struggled to continue speaking. "I should have checked. I should have known to look," she wailed.

"Ali, listen to me. It is *not* your fault. And Daydream had a choice too. She could have called me when you were in trouble, instead of waiting until she was exhausted. She wanted to save you herself. It was her last gift to you. Her way to let you know how much she loves you."

Ali pulled her knees close to her body and wrapped her arms around her legs. Her eyes pierced the waves at the spot she'd last seen her beloved friend, just in case. Slowly the sun dropped in the west, coloring the waves a brilliant vermilion and glorious pink. And Ali knew in her heart Daydream wasn't coming home ever again.

Her stiff muscles protested as she stood and turned away. She followed Angelica over the rocks and walked along the black sand beside the older girl. They stopped where Daydream's hoof prints entered the water. Ali looked down and circled one with her toe. Tears ran from her eyes again. Then she looked at

Angelica. Angelica's eyes sparkled golden in the dying light.

"Thanks for staying with me," Ali said quietly.

"I wish I could take the pain away," Angelica said and wrapped her arms around Ali one more time.

Ali hugged her back, fiercely. "Me too," she said and smiled through her tears. When the two pulled away from each other, Ali added, "And thanks for saving me. Again."

"It will not always hurt like this, Ali. I promise."

"I know," said Ali, even though she didn't. "I'll be okay."

"Are you sure?"

Ali nodded her head. Another tear ran down her cheek. "I better get home. Mom will be worried. How am I going to tell her?" Her words choked to a stop again.

"You will find the right words," Angelica said gently.

Ali only nodded again. She would have to. "Good bye, Angelica" she whispered.

"Good bye."

Ali turned and walked slowly along the black sand toward the trail. The moon was rising in front of her, perched on the edge of the volcano like a huge shiny balloon. The light danced across Daydream's hoof prints and slid silver along the marks made by the boat when Ali had so innocently pushed it to the water's edge. There was a flash of light from behind her and Ali looked back. The beach was deserted. Angelica was gone. She cast her eyes over the moonlit waters one more time.

"I love you, Daydream," she whispered. She held still and listened the way Crystal's foals always stopped

160

and listened for their dam after calling her, but there was no response. With a sob, Ali turned back to the trail.

She was almost to the horse pasture when she felt *something* – an energy spinning beside her. At first she was hardly aware of it, her grief was so consuming, but when she finally noticed it, she knew who it was. Daydream! She *had* come back. Ali stopped and put her hand out. She felt the energy brushing against her fingertips.

"Daydream," she whispered, filled with wonder. She closed her eyes and concentrated on feeling Daydream's presence. Her eyes sprung open when something solid touched the back of her hand. A white petal was falling to the ground. The petal of a wild moonflower. Then the energy moved away.

Ali followed it the best she could. It took her a minute to think of looking down. The flower petals glowed soft in the moonlight. Ali hurried along the moonflower trail, the sounds of the night pulsing around her. Crystal and Rhythm waited for her in the pasture near the house. They whinnied to her as she drew near.

Ali gasped when she saw the two horses clearly in the lunar light. Their manes and forelocks were white with flowers – moonflowers – meticulously braided into their long, flowing hair. The intoxicating scent of white petals capered about them and Ali felt Daydream's energy again, swirling round her. Crystal nickered and Rhythm nuzzled Ali's shoulder. Then he reached out and lipped a flower from her dark hair. Ali laughed out loud in amazement and threw an arm around each warm neck.

161

"I understand, Daydream," she said to the night sky. "You *are* still here. You're still part of us, through Crystal and Rhythm." She looked deep into Rhythm's eyes, then turned to Crystal. "And through Crystal's baby too." Her hand stroked the silken neck and the young mare nickered gently.

"Life goes on, doesn't it girl?" Ali whispered. "A new foal for you. A healed shoulder for Rhythm." She glanced at the house. Light poured from the kitchen window and Ali could see Peter's truck parked in the driveway. "Probably a new husband for my mom – and a stepfather for me."

Ali loosened one of the flower stems braided into Crystal's forelock, held the white blossom up to the moon and looked into its luminous center. "And a whole new world for Daydream," she whispered. "Things we can't even imagine right now. But they're good things. Very good things." She reached out and took another flower, this one from Rhythm's forelock.

"What's this?" A faint tinkle. A warmth on her fingers. Another necklace. Angelica had left her another necklace. With new tears in her eyes, Ali put the necklace over her head.

"Thank you, Angelica," she whispered. The wind sighed around her for a second, then fell silent.

Daydream's energy was dissipating now. Ali could feel it. She patted Crystal and Rhythm on their necks, then watched them as they wandered away. The glow of the moonflowers faded into the darkness.

"Come on, Daydream," she said, her voice full of tears. "Walk with me one more time." Then she turned toward the house, the two flowers clutched in her hand.

162

Daydream, she understands. She will always love you and remember you with only gladness in her heart. As will I. Goodbye, my love, my Daydream, until I am with you again. Go with grace and beauty, wild moonflower horse.

Nugget. I hear you. Your panic screams to me, your grief and horror resonate through me. Hold firm. I am coming!

What will happen next?

Please turn the page
for a sneak preview
of the next book

Gold Fever

Available at:

www.ponybooks.com

On their annual horseback camping trip into the
Canadian wilderness, Karlie and her dad run
into a bit of unexpected trouble, trouble that
quickly turns terrifying. Karlie's dad is
attacked and horribly injured by a murderer,
then as he and Karlie escape, they are
separated.

Karlie knows she must find her dad and get
him to a hospital as fast as she can, and she's
confident she'll succeed as long as she uses all
her survival and tracking skills. The only
question, will she find him in time?

Then she discovers she's not the only one
looking for him. The armed murderer is
looking too – for her dad *and* for her.

www.ponybooks.com

CPSIA information can be obtained at www.ICGtesting.com
Printed in the USA
LVOW121631020312

271367LV00008B/46/P